BRIGID

AND THE RAVEN KING

by

Gez Taylor

Jazz-Fusion Books

First published March 2024
Jazz-Fusion Books
Gravesend Cottage
Torpoint
Cornwall PL11 2LX
United Kingdom

ISBN: 978-1-9993273-7-8

Brigid / Tsun - Spirit of Spring

5

An Odyssey

Seán O'Malley was just sixteen when he walked away from his family and the booley settlement on Sliabh Mór (Slievemore Mountain). Life on Achill Island for Seán had ended abruptly. All alone, he walked along dirt roads and the shores of dark lakes. To start a new life, he was following the coast of County Mayo, a new life that had to begin in Sligo Town.

Relentless hard rain had been on him all day. When darkness fell Seán took refuge beneath a solitary hawthorn tree. Lying on a bed of leaves, he closed his eyes in the hope of going to sleep. Rain, hunger and memories would not allow it. Instead, in a waking dream, he relived the leaving of Sliabh Mór. It began with a memory that made him smile.

On the horizon the sun was setting as Seán walked down the mountainside with Niamh, his childhood sweetheart. Along with the other young ones from the village, they had been tending the scraggy cows in the field above. Being some way ahead of the others, Seán and Niamh dared to hold hands.

Scared and worried, Niamh said to Seán,

Jaysus, Seán, this hunger's unbearable and I have the pain in me. It breaks my heart to see the auld ones suffering and dying. That Yaller Indian they'd be selling us, tis hard to keep down, sure it's no use at all. What'll become of us? (Yaller Indian was one of many names given to Indian Meal. This was unground maize that was bought from America by the British Government. It was a cheap dietary substitute that was sold to the people in need. Digesting it was difficult and caused dysentery.)

Seán replied,

I've no idea, Niamh. If the potatoes fail again this year, it'll be even worse, and we'll not be able to pay the rent.

What about the herd? Will they take it from us?

Seán looked away when he answered.

They will a stór (my love). It's just a matter of time.

Drawing near to their village they looked down on a mile-long row of rooftops. These stone cottages were their homes every summer. Smoke from the peat fires rose from the heather roofs to greet them.

Looking beyond the smoke, they could see the men from the village walking up the mountain road. Each one carried a bag of Indian meal to feed his family.

God love us and save us Seán, will ye look at how slow they walk. It's like they've the weight of the world on their backs. They must be exhausted, what with working on the roads and the bogs just so's we can stay alive. And after that they'd be walking ten miles and back again just to be buying that poxy Yaller Indian.

Sure, it'll be our mammys working with 'em soon and then na páistí (the children) after that.

The sons and daughters gathered at the end of the row of houses to wait for their fathers to come up the road. There was no shouting or laughing as there would once have been. Instead, each child went over to meet their da in silence.

After saying goodbye to Niamh, Seán walked over to Paud, his father. As always when he saw any of his children, he had a light in his eyes. He put his arm around Seán's shoulder and they walked a little way before

Paud said,

Let's stop here son and look over to the sea. I want to talk with you for a while.

Taking in the smell of the heather and the sea they stood for just a moment in silence. Then Seán asked,

Do you think our Micheál will be alright da?

Micheál was Seán's elder brother who had recently accepted a ticket from the landlord to set sail for Canada. Seán was worried about him because of the frightening stories about the coffin ships, especially as one had recently sunk just outside Westport harbour.

Ah, course he'll be fine lad. He'd be strong enough for that trip and after getting there he'll find work. Then, please God, he'll be sending money back to us. These are terrible times and it's not just the hunger. There'll be worse things coming to us.

How so father?

The landlords are wanting us off the land. With the law on their side, they'll be able to do it. Sure, the evictions have already started. All over Mayo it's been happening and now, God help us, it's starting here on Achill. They've brought out laws that say if you owe rent then the landlord's able to evict you. Of course, we're all to be owing money soon. To top that boy, the landlords are taking crops and livestock. They're sending grain, meat and dairy to England while we're having to buy that Indian Meal. As they take the food so they're bringing over thousands of soldiers to guard its removal. Ah but that's the go boy, I'd say that's the go.

The Protestant mission up the road in Dugort is starting to buy lots of land. Yer man, Edward Nangle is after telling people he'll give 'em food and work if they renounce their faith and become Protestants. Nobody here's given into that yet but when things get worse I think some will leave the faith just to stay alive. Jaysus, I hope it never comes to that.

The other day, the bailiffs, police and army gave a visit to Finsheen. They threw the people out and Jaysus didn't they even take the pots and pans from out of their houses. After that they stole the little bit of livestock and food the poor divils had. When that was done they set fire to the roofs and turned the families out into the fields. They told 'em to never return.

Billy came across 'em walking across the fields. He said the poor souls looked lost. They told him all that had gone on. There must be a hundred and fifty of 'em, and all of 'em will be sleeping out in the cold. God bless 'em, they'd be having to walk forty miles to the workhouse in Westport. I'd be worried about the auld ones. Sure, most of 'em won't make it.

Upset by what his father had just told him Seán said,

That's terrible father. Could they not go to family, to friends nearby or even stay up here?

No Seán, this new law they have says if these people get refuge in another house then that house'll be burnt down and the people in it will be evicted as well.

Just as he said that someone outside one of the cottages shouted.

Look, come out everyone, come and look!

As the families came out, Seán and his da looked down to the beach road. Moving quickly towards Keel, the neighbouring village, was a band of riders and a horse and cart. Most of the riders wore red coats so they knew they were soldiers. Bailiffs and the Royal Irish Constabulary would be the other riders. The whole population of the settlement were out by the wall looking down on the road to see what was going to happen. Nobody spoke, they just watched, wide eyed in the hope that this was not what they were all expecting.

The riders and carts turned off the road and went down the dirt road to the small group of cottages. It was not long before smoke billowed from the roofs of the cottages. There soon followed flames that leapt high into the sky. Many of the people that looked over the wall were crying and making the sign of the cross. They were overcome by anger, fear and sadness. That burning village by the sea was home to relatives and lifelong friends.

Seán's memory left that sad moment. It moved to his home two days later. It was early morning and still dark outside. His mother kindled the fire while his father and brother got ready to leave for work. The two little ones were covered with hessian sacks as they were still asleep on the stone seats. There was only one room in the cottage so Seán's sister and younger brother were used to sleeping through noise. Paud whispered to Seán,

Let's step outside the house, I want to have that talk with you that we didn't finish.

Standing by the wall, they looked at the reflection of the yellow moon on the sea.

Paud spoke quietly,

It breaks my heart to tell you this son but I have to do it now. Time's running out on us.

Something ominous in the tone of his voice made Seán feel uneasy.

I have to tell you son, like your brother, ye have to be leaving us. I am so sorry Seán, I wish that you didn't have to.

Seán was shocked and scared. For the first time in his life, he saw tears in his father's eyes.

Jaysus da, why?

You've seen how it is after last year's blight, the evictions and the hunger. We'll be digging up this year's crop soon. If the potatoes have the blight again we'll all be finished. The landlord's agent could well be sending his friends round to take our livestock to pay our rent. Then if we're not able to pay the next time they will turf us out so. All that's left Seán is for you to leave and find work so you can send money back. That way, please God, we may hold on to our animals and stay alive.

Da steadied Seán's hands that were shaking.

Your brother will be after leaving soon, but you Seán must leave even before that.

But where would I go da? There's no work on the island.

Dear God, I never thought I'd be saying this Seán but I'm asking you to take the Queen's shilling. In a few days the Royal Irish are recruiting up in Sligo.

It's a big thing I'm asking son but there's nothing else.

There's no work anywhere. The landlords have every man working on their estates for just enough to buy that Indian meal.

Seán was scared of losing everything that he knew and loved. Feeling a stream of emotions and unable to speak he looked at the ground in despair.

Paud put his arm around him and said,

I know we've been through hard times son, but Jaysus, this is far worse. This meal they sell us is making the auld ones and the wains ill. If you and Michael were able to send us money, then we might have a chance. God help us, your grandad would turn in his grave if he knew you'd be joining the British army.

Seán answered,

Will they be having me evicting tenants? I couldn't be doing that to our own people.

Naw Seán, they don't use the Royal Irish for that. Sure, it's the York and Lancaster regiment that they use. So, will you do it lad?

Of course, I'll do what you ask da, but God willing, I'll be back soon.

Beneath the hawthorn tree Seán's memories faded into the darkness and the only sound now was the persistent rain. Lying beneath the oilskin coat Seán closed his eyes. Once more he hoped to relive those precious moments. Instead, a clap of thunder forced him to open his eyes and sit up. Complete darkness surrounded him. Lightning suddenly flashed to bring a brief moment of clarity. Nearby, Seán saw an animal standing in the shadows between the trees. When the darkness returned, Seán laid back down. After a while, the rain ceased and a thrush started to sing. Looking into the dark night, Seán saw a small golden ball of light. It was shimmering on the ground like a tiny fallen star. Overwhelmed by its presence, Seán somehow felt less lonely. Within seconds the bird ceased singing and the golden light vanished.

After that, the night before his departure returned in cold reality. The able-bodied ones from the village were sitting in the field around a fire, while his uncle Brendan played Farewell to Music on his fiddle. It was one of Seán's favourite O'Carolan tunes. Sadly no one had the energy to dance. Brendan was ancient but still remembered the music his grand-father, Séamus had taught him. Turlough O'Carolan, the blind harpist, had come to their village once and had played music with Séamus. After learning many songs from him, Séamus in return shared the music from Achill with Turlough. There was Seán-nós (unaccompanied singing) from a few of the old ones and of course stories were told. (O'Carolan was a blind harpist and composer. Many of his songs have survived in words and music. He was an itinerant harpist who travelled on horseback with his harp all over Ireland.)

Niamh was sitting close to Seán. Around the fire were his friends and family. Áine, his beloved grandmother, sat across the fire from Seán. As he sipped the poitín Seán began to feel as if he was at his own wake. Smoke from the fire drifted across the blue moon and as Seán watched he noticed movement. It was a tiny black speck spiralling downwards between the smoke and the moon. All the time it was getting nearer. As it got close Seán realised that it was a bird.

As it descended through the smoke Seán knew that it was his friend. Silently, Cormac landed next to him.

Áine said,

Ah, good God, tis himself, your own fiach dubh (raven). Do ye remember when ye found Cormac fallen from the nest on the Sídh (fairy mound)? You were after bringing him to meself and we reared him between us. I remember you telling me grandma that he'd been given to me by the Daoine Sídhe (Faerie folk).

I'll tell ya now boy, there's more. Cormac was brought back into this world just so he could help you in yer travels. In another life he was the high king of Ireland and he went by the name of Cormac Mac Airt. He ruled from the Hill of Tara with the help of Fionn Mac Cumhaill and the Fianna. So there ya have it boy. Cormac has come back to be yer own Rí Mbranáin [Raven King]. Through all yer travels he'll protect ya and be yer connection with the Tuatha de Danann. So that, me darlin' boy, is why the Aos Sí (people of the mounds) gave him to ya.

Áine was tired and became quiet. Bowing her head, she stared into the fire. Seán was astounded to hear what she had just told him, but he was also worried about her.

Turning to Cormac Seán stroked his head and whispered,

Will you ask the Aos Sí to look after grandma for me?

The raven nodded.

Despite being tired, Áine's spirit was still strong. After a while she raised her head and called across the fire,

Seán, can ya hear me looking at ya?

This made Seán laugh, as it was something she would often say to him when he was little.

God, I'm sorry grandma, I didn't hear you. What is it?

I'm for me leaba (bed) Seán. Will ye take me home?

After standing up Seán reached out and helped Áine to her feet. She said goodnight to everyone and touched Seán's mother, Maeve's shoulder as she passed her. They walked over to her place and after giving him a hug Áine said,

There's something I must tell you before ye go.

They sat on the old chairs that were outside and Áine began.

You've seen how the Protestants down there at the mission say the Catholics are all heathens. Well both lots, the Catholic and the Protestant clergy, see us as peasants and heathens if we don't abide by their story. Between the priests and the English aristocracy, our history and freedom has been stolen and nearly forgotten. Remember this Seán, long before these people came here our ancestors had an understanding of this world, the seasons, the wild and the other side. But the wisdom of the druids has been written out of our history and much has been lost. Soon they'll get rid of everything we remember of that time by taking away our language. When the old knowledge is gone then the world will be in danger. I don't know how, but you'll be important to this knowledge. You are about to make a journey that is much more than joining the army.

Seán knew that he would remember what his grandmother had just told him but right then he did not understand. Knowing this Áine kissed his cheek and said,

See ye in the morning boy, codladh sámh (sleep well).

His dream then jumped to the following morning. Seán's da had just woken him and he was surprised to see that everyone in the house was already up. Not knowing what to say, Seán started to pack his bag with the Indian meal that some of the neighbours had given him. Maeve watched him in silence. She wanted to jump up and hold on to him and never let him leave. Instead, she rekindled the fire. Even the children were awake because they knew they must say goodbye to their brother.

The moment had arrived for Seán to part from his family and friends.

Kevin and Lizzie, his little brother and sister, were sobbing and Seán tried to comfort them. Paud knelt down and hugged them all. After a while Seán went over to his ma. She held him for a long time. All the while she was crying. Eventually she managed to speak,

Jaysus, son, I'll be missing ya. You'll come back won't you?

Trying to hide his uncertainty he replied,

Of course I will ma.

She held him for the last time and whispered in his ear,

Don't be afraid son, Brigid will always be with you.

As he did not understand this, Seán did not reply. Instead, he stepped back, smiled at her and wiped the tears from her eyes.

Remember that I love you mam. My spirit is within you.

Unable to say the words good-bye to her, Seán turned away. Kneeling down, he gathered his little brother and sister into his arms. The children were shaking as they held onto him. Gently Seán whispered,

Whisht now, don't be crying on me. Ye must look after mam and da when Micheál and meself have gone.

After kissing them he stood up to speak to his da,

Where's Micheál?

He's along the mountain road with the donkey and cart. He'll be taking yerself to the mainland. I have some things for you lad.

First he gave Seán a pouch of milk. For the bad weather he gave him a big oilskin coat with a sugan (straw rope) to tie around the middle. Handing Seán a small map he said,

You might need this as well son. I've drawn it out for ya. Tis the way you'll need to follow the coast without climbing over the mountains. Take care of yerself. Sure, we're all proud of you boy.

Seán was too upset to answer.

In a quiet and faltering voice Paud said,

Come on now, we'll see ye off from the door. Paud put his arms around Seán. After hugging him, Paud kissed Seán on the cheek. He stood back and they shook hands. Paud held onto Seán's hand and said,

Slán agus beannacht Dé a mhac (Goodbye and God bless son).

Closing his eyes, Seán just nodded and turned to leave. Maeve was crying helplessly. In a final blessing she sprinkled holy water over Seán as he went out of the door.

Outside the whole village had turned out to see him off. Cormac, his raven, was sitting on the wall next to Áine. After stroking Cormac's head, Seán turned to his grandma. As they hugged, she said to Seán,

I have a sadness in me for I'll not see you again. At least not in this life. Sure I'll miss ya.

Distraught, he held onto her. Seán kissed Áine before saying goodbye.

It took Seán an age to walk along that dirt road. All the people he had grown up with were there shaking his hand. Just like his mother, a person from each household sprinkled holy water over Seán. As he passed along, he heard many of them say, God bless you Seán. He had not gone far when he heard his mother wailing from their doorway. The piercing sound cut into Seán's heart. She was keening. It was a mournful cry that he had heard at many funerals recently. Seán turned around and saw his mam with her shawl covering her face. His da had his arms around her and his head on her shoulder. As Seán moved along the path some of the other women took up the same cry. Never in his life had he felt such sorrow as he walked through this gauntlet of love.

Seán was concerned because his Niamh was nowhere to be seen. After passing the last cottage, he stood alone. No one had followed him. After walking for a while, he saw Niamh standing where the dirt track met the mountain road. As the keening filled the air and their hearts with pain, they held onto each other. Speaking slowly, Niamh quietly stuttered her words,

I really thought we'd be married one day, Seán. It makes me sad because I don't think that'll happen now.

Ah now, Niamh a chuisle mo chroí (my darling), I promise you we shall be together one day.

It was then that they kissed for the very first time. After that kiss, Seán turned around and walked away. There were no more words. Only now did he let his own tears fall.

At that point his dream left him once more. Opening his eyes, he saw that the rain had ceased and a bright dawn was breaking. A mist lying close to the ground surrounded him. Sloping upwards and beyond the mist lay green fields and woods that were not yet defined as they were still waking. Faint blue mountains rose up in the far distance. In the green fields he saw the golden ball once again. Birds were singing as he stared at the golden light moving towards the mountains. Eventually it vanished and was replaced by a small white deer. Instinctively, Seán knew that it was the creature he had half seen amongst the trees. Contrasting with the misty fields, the deer was bright and clear. Vibrant and motionless, the creature turned its head to look at Seán. Even though there was some distance between them, Seán could hear the deer's heartbeat. It was as if it were standing next to him. Intrigued, Seán kept as still as the deer. His own heart began to beat just as loudly and in unison with the creature. The connection lasted for just a few moments before the deer turned and ran.

Seán felt a new strength inside him. Over the birds' song his mother whispered in his ear, as she had on the morning he left,

Don't be afraid son. Brigid will always be with you.

Turning around, Seán hoped to see his mother sitting beside him. No one was there and he was still alone.

Brigid was a name he knew well. His childhood was full of stories told by the old ones about Ireland before St. Patrick, powerful stories of druids, gods and heroes. All that Seán could remember about Brigid was that she was the Spiorad an Earraigh [Spirit of Spring] goddess with connections to wells, poetry and healing. She also belonged to a tribe called the Tuatha de Danann that came to Ireland from the other world. Stories of Brigid and the other gods in Seán's childhood became entwined with the stories of saints and the Bible. These stories were told to the children in school by teachers and priests in English, the new language. (The British Government had allowed Catholic schools for the first time ever 15 years before the famine. Only English was allowed to be spoken. This meant that while the older generations spoke Irish the younger generation were learning to speak English.)

Like the other children in the village, he grew up believing in both mythologies. It became even more confusing when he learnt of Edward

Nangle, the Protestant mission in Dugort who wanted to teach an alternative Christianity.

As Seán was going over all of this in his mind he remembered that there was a Saint Brigid in the Catholic stories to match the Brigid of old. He also remembered that the priest had told them that it was a sin to believe in the Protestant God or the druid Gods.

When the mist cleared Seán continued his walk. He felt comforted after having heard his mother's voice and seen that golden light and the deer. Seán followed a narrow path between ploughed fields when he saw desperate people in rags searching hedgerows for food. They did not notice him as he walked silently past them.

A few hours later Seán met a few men and women working on the road. He got to speak to them and each one of them had a story to tell of the hardships they were going through or the evictions that were happening in Mayo. Some said they had seen friends or relatives buried without a priest or a coffin. They told him that some families in the remote parts were discovered lying where they had died. One man told him of mounted troops escorting food for the landlords to the ports in Sligo and Westport for export to England. All of them were angry at this crime that was being committed against them and their families. Seán decided that it was best not to tell them the purpose of his journey.

As he neared Sligo he saw the Atlantic framed by mountains and it made him feel at home. A farm labourer driving a horse and hay wagon pulled up alongside Seán and asked if he would like a lift into Sligo. Seán climbed aboard and noticed from the corner of his eye that in the back of the cart were bundles of dirty rags. With a smile the driver told Seán that his name was Gearóid and shook his hand

Just before the horse began to move, Seán heard a groan in the back of the cart. Turning around he realised that the rags were the clothes of men, women and children. Because these people of the land were so pale and gaunt, Seán at first thought they were ghosts. Some were separated from the huddled group, and lying motionless on the floor of the cart. Seán was upset to see them. Nearest to Seán was a woman whose head was bowed down. Inside her shawl Seán could see a small child looking up at him from out of the darkness. Her unblinking eyes were even darker. In the centre of each eye there shone a bright golden light. Seán was transfixed.

After a while he pulled himself away and turning to Gearóid asked,

Who are these people? Why are they in your cart?

Sure the poor divils are from a village near me. They're off to board a ship that's waiting in the harbour.

Do you mean one of the coffin ships?

The labourer frowned at Seán and whispered,

I do lad, but don't be saying that out loud again, they might hear you. Our landlord is after paying me to take his wretched tenants to the docks as he's paid for them to go to Canada. Tis a way of clearing 'em off the land. Sure, it doesn't cost the landlord much as they're auld cargo ships. They have no place fer passengers. Tis just cargo these people are. They'll be kept like cattle in the ship's hold. Wasn't me own wife's family taken last week to Canada on a ship called The Carricks. Jaysus, it was in no fit state and it should have been scrapped. Sure, it should never have been sailing the seas let alone carrying people. God knows if we'll ever see 'em again. It broke her heart to see 'em go.

When he finished talking Gearóid made the sign of the cross. Seán could not bear to look at the families behind him, knowing that it could soon be his own people being taken away. He wished that he could offer them food, but his supply of Indian meal was gone.

The countryside was glorious, but the progress was sombre. The large number of solemn families that walked on the road increased as they approached Sligo town. Seán asked Gearóid about these ragged people.

Why are all these people going into the town?

They're hoping to be taken into the workhouse in the north of the town. I'm told it's an awful place. They separate the men from their families and many people die in the fever hospital. These people are desperate Seán. The poor souls go there in the hope they'd be getting a scrap of food. May God have mercy on them.

All that Seán could say was, Jaysus, Mary and Joseph. Then he became quiet again.

When they entered the broad streets of the town, Seán was overwhelmed by the size of the big houses. He was fascinated to see the well-dressed gentry walking up and down the streets alongside the broken country people.

Gearóid stopped the cart by the side of a river and said to Seán,

You're near the green where you'll sign up Seán. I'll leave you here now as I must be off to the docks. Before I go, I want to tell you that I was given a task today.

Seán looked confused. How so Gearóid?

Well now, I was after being told to pick you up on the road and take you to this river, the Garavogue. I'm also to tell ya that, although you've come here to join the army, the real purpose is that you are to begin a lifelong journey, an odyssey, I was told, that will carry on through your lives beyond this one. There'll be others on the same journey, some with different paths, but all of them will share the same destination as yerself. The choice is yours, mind. The recruiting tent is on the green just beyond these buildings, and it's there that it'll all begin. But if you want, you can walk away. Stay here awhile, spend time by this grand river before you decide. Sure, the Garavogue will help you make up your mind. Slán Seán. May the spirit of Brigid be with you.

There it was, that name again, Brigid. Seán was so overcome by what he had just heard that he didn't think to ask Gearóid who had given him the task of picking him up on the road. Instead Seán replied

Thank you Gearóid, I hope one day I'll understand what you've told me.

They shook hands and Seán climbed down onto the road. He looked once more at the people huddled in the back of the cart. Some of them seemed more awake now and were staring at the river. The child that was hidden in her mother's shawl was looking at him again, but now he was able to see her emaciated face more clearly. Her dark sunken eyes were still reflecting that golden light. The contrast between that pale haunted face and the brightness in her eyes was something that Seán would never forget.

The snap of the reins, the cart lurching forward, and the sound of the horse's hooves broke the spell. The distraction caused Seán to turn his head away from the girl but as the cart passed, he looked at her once more. Bowing her head, she opened her mother's shawl with her tiny hands to reveal the cause of the reflection in her eyes. It was a small golden ball of light. Raising her head, she smiled and Seán knew that there was hope for her. He watched the wagon as it moved over the cobbled street towards the docks.

Turning, Seán walked over the road to the river. While leaning on the railings, he began to think about what he had just experienced as well as his future. Seán's mind was racing and he felt weak with hunger. The sky had become cloudy, and the river turned grey and turbulent.

Looking down on the water, Seán saw a watery vision of what was happening at the quayside. The coffin ship that the girl and her family were on was just leaving the quayside. Watching the departing ship from the shore was a solitary figure. Only this frail old man was there to say goodbye. Holding a fiddle by his side he slowly brought it to his chin. The slow air that he played crossed over to the families and Seán could hear every painfully sad note. Like motionless dark shadows, the families stood on deck. They looked like figures carved from the ship's black timbers. Abruptly, the vision and sound were swallowed by the turbulent river. The tune played by the old man was familiar to Seán. It was often sung at the wakes back home and known as The Parting Glass. On that day, that bittersweet farewell at the docks and the dark eyes of the little girl became etched into his memory forever.

Seán continued to watch the dark rippling grey water and wondered if the river was offering him an alternative. Perhaps he could sink to the bottom and never come back up. Sunshine suddenly beamed through the dark clouds. Immediately the clouds dispersed, and the light transformed the dark river into a long glistening sheet of silver. Seán's impulse to drown left with the clouds. Hunger pains returned and reminded him that he had no way of getting any food. His choices were stark. To take the Queen's shilling or join those on the road to the workhouse.

Gearóid's words and his father's bidding about the odyssey helped Seán to resolve any doubts. Choosing to join an army that he despised, Seán left the river and walked up the street to the green.

THE QUEEN'S SHILLING

After a short walk Seán turned the corner of the street. Soon he came to a gap in the buildings and turned to look into a Square. There was a grandeur in front of Seán that he had never seen before. Elegant Georgian houses surrounded a perfect lawn. Pitched in the centre of that lawn was the recruiting tent. Fluttering in the breeze above it, on a white pole was the Union flag. Feeling apprehensive, Seán approached the tent. Two soldiers in uniform with rifles sloped on their shoulders were standing to attention outside the tent. In front of them were two other soldiers sitting at a long table.

As Seán neared the table one of the soldiers looked over his shoulder towards the tent and called out,

Sergeant major, another recruit coming up.

Just as Seán arrived at the table a tall officer came out of the tent. Looking down at Seán with cold intimidating eyes, the sergeant major sneered. With an English accent he shouted,

Well, what do you want, boy?

Seán was not intimidated. He had experienced this tone before from his landlord's English agent.

I want to join up mister. Take the Queen's shilling.

The sergeant major looked at Seán with disdain. He didn't like being called mister and he certainly didn't like the Irish.

Without making eye contact, the sergeant major shouted,

Sit there and sign your name. That's if you can write.

I'm able to do that mister, said Seán

One of the soldiers said in a Mayo accent,

Sit here lad, we have the papers for yerself.

Within the next 10-minutes Seán committed himself to serve in the Royal Irish Regiment for the next twenty-one years without realising it. He could sign his name, but he could not read or write very well.

After Seán had finished signing the papers the soldier said,

That's grand, now take yerself into the tent and the sergeant major will see to ya.

Inside the big tent Seán saw thirty young men sitting quietly and looking nervous. The sergeant major took Seán over to a well-dressed man sitting at a desk.

This is the magistrate, said the sergeant major. Stand to attention and swear allegiance to the Queen on that Bible.

After Seán had sworn allegiance, the Sergeant Major looked down at him saying,

From now on boy, you call me sergeant major, not bloody mister, you piece of scum. Now sit over there with the other peasants.

The degradation had begun.

Soon after all the recruits were taken to the barracks. Training began immediately. In the following weeks Seán began to learn about army life. Training consisted mainly of drilling, rifle practice and learning how to charge with a bayonet. During this time, it became evident that the most important thing to learn was that you must obey and never question an order. If they did anything wrong, they were told that they would be subjected to flogging. The maximum strokes would be three hundred.

On the first day Seán was told that he would be paid a shilling a day. This would be decreased by stoppages of up to half a shilling for his daily rations, clothing and medical services. Seán and a lot of the other recruits found it hard to adapt to being shouted at. They were insulted with constant obscenities from what they were told were their superiors. Seán knew that this would become easier with time. On the positive side, they were being fed. All of the recruits were Irish and all of the officers above the rank of sergeant were English. There was a camaraderie between the one hundred and fifty new soldiers. Most of these young men were from the West Coast. All of them felt uncomfortable in their new role as soldiers.

Seán made friends with the other recruits in his overcrowded hut. Within a week Seán had made a particularly strong bond of friendship with two of them. There was Conor from Sligo and Billy from Kerry. All of them instinctively knew that if they weren't separated their friendship would last a long time.

In the evenings everyone was exhausted. Still, they played cards, sang songs and told stories. It was a joy for Seán to be able to laugh once more. This was the first two weeks of Seán's career in the army. After that training, the recruits and officers boarded a train to the garrison town of Clonmel in Tipperary. In the Kickham Barracks on the edge of the town they joined the 1st Battalion of the Royal Irish Regiment.

On arrival at the Barracks the new recruits were split up and put with various platoons of the regular soldiers. Fortunately, Seán, Conor and Billy were placed in the same platoon. The troops were friendly and made the transition for the newcomers as easy as possible. Seán was told that the purpose of the regiment was not to assist in the clearances. Instead, they were to guard food that came into and across county Waterford. The food supplies came from all over Ireland. Seán and his friends were now part of a body of five hundred soldiers. They marched in front of vast herds of cattle and sheep. Sometimes they would be on barges carrying oats, barley and dairy products.

Various regiments moved the food from all over Ireland. They accompanied food supplies into County Waterford. Destined for England via the port of Youghal, they entered the county by going over the Knock-mealdown mountains or through the town of Fermoy. The food needed to be protected from the starving people who worked on the tenant farms that the food had come from. The need increased as people became more desperate.

Sometimes the troops gave protection to produce coming from local farms and estates. On one such occasion, Seán, Billy and Conor were with other troops taking a barge full of corn from a farm just outside the town of Tallow. At first light the barge moved quietly down the mist-covered river Bride. Upright and alert, the soldiers were sitting in the bow with loaded rifles resting on their shoulders. Seán leaned forward and asked Corporal Phelan, the officer in charge, why one of the soldiers was steering the barge, adding,

I thought it'd be one of the locals doing that job.

The corporal answered,

Two days ago this barge was turned around. It was sent back to the farm by a mob and the boatman was threatened. This grain has to get to Youghal by midday before the ship sets sail. We have to make sure it gets there.

Just as the corporal turned back a stone hit the bow. A constant stream of stones followed from a group of men and women on the riverbank. Desperate and angry, they shouted abuse as they hurled stones. Raising his rifle, the corporal fired a shot over their heads. It was an anxious moment. Nobody in the barge spoke as the tension mounted. Tensions dissipated when the crowd turned around and walked back into the woods.

Further along, as they approached the much larger Blackwater river, the mist began to rise over its banks. It continued to spread until the fields were covered in a low, white cloud, whilst the river itself became clear. After passing Lismore Castle and going under the nearby bridge, they were disturbed to see ghosts in the distance. Then, to their surprise as they drew nearer, they realised that what they were seeing were not ghosts, but families of gaunt, silent and hungry people. However, it would not be long before they would become ghosts that would never leave these fields and hedgerows.

Remaining perfectly still, the families stared in disbelief at the food being taken away by an armed vessel. Even though they were too weak to react, the pain and sadness on their faces conveyed their living hell to the Irish soldiers. Those faces would haunt the men for the rest of their lives.

Seeing the emaciated children with grass-stained mouths prompted Joe to say,

Begod, these poor souls have no food, no homes and nowhere to go. May God have mercy on 'em.

Conor asked,

The workhouse, can they not go there?

Joe answered,

Sure, there's one here in Lismore. Many of 'em would rather die than go in there. The government says that if a tenant farmer has more than a quarter of an acre of land, he'd not be getting help or a place in the work-house. Believe me lads, they're better off in the fields picking berries than going in those places.

How so?

Dark satanic places, that's what they are, boy. They split the families. The men don't see their children or wives. Sure, they're all dying of hunger and disease in there. After dying the poor divils are buried in mass graves. They use a sliding coffin over and over again.

Seán interrupted.

Jaysus, what the hell are mass graves?

They're big, unmarked pits where they bury all the dead ones from the workhouse. Not even a marker to say who is in there. Sure, there's one mass grave near the church in Lismore. Some of these people could have lived if they'd renounced their faith. The Protestant church offers food in exchange for their souls, but they would rather die. God help them.

At this Seán remembered the Protestant missionary near his home that did exactly the same thing - food for souls.

Joe continued,

I'm from around here, so I know families that are in that workhouse right now. Even Hessie, me own grandma, is in there, God help her. And I know families that are at the bottom of that pit as well. Even though they're martyrs, the church allows them to be put in unmarked graves in land that's not even consecrated. It's as if they're criminals. Sure, their only crime is to be poor.

As he said that he made the sign of the cross, and so did Conor, Billy and Seán.

Looking back at the last family they had passed, Conor said,

You know what we're doing here boys is wrong. There's hunger everywhere and we're helping to take the food off 'em. It's not just the potato blight that's killing our people, it's the food from the farms and estates that's being denied to them.

Joe replied,

You're right lad, may God forgive us. But we have to obey orders, there's no choice.

Seán now understood why most of the troops in the barracks seemed to be sad.

Things are going to get worse. People are starting to organise 'emselves to get food. Some of the soldiers have been telling me there's been riots. They said crowds armed with sticks, spades and hammers were down at Fishers Mill in Pilltown. They were after wanting the price of the meal to be lowered so they could afford it. At the same time there was a big crowd attacking the Magistrates Court in Clashmore. They were after Lord Stuart de Decies, but he was after getting away in his carriage. And, there's talk of the Young Ireland movement coming here. Sure, if they do there'll be more arms brought into the County. God, I wish we were back in India, at least it wasn't our own people we were chasin'.

The barge arrived in time at the docks. The corn was loaded onto the ship whilst the soldiers stood on guard in a line. Corporal Phelan was talking to one of the dock workers when a mounted soldier rode at speed along the dockside and stopped alongside him. All of the soldiers in the line were watching as the rider dismounted. After saluting, he spoke to the Corporal. Within minutes, the corporal came striding over shouting orders, telling the soldiers to get into the wagons that were waiting nearby. As he climbed up onto the seat alongside the driver, he shouted to the men sitting in the back.

We must leave now, there's rioting and looting in Dungarvan. They're trying to break into the grain stores on the quay.

The horseman took the lead and the horse and cart tried to keep up. On arriving at the quay side in Dungarvan, the Irish troops disembarked in time to see the 1st Royal Dragoons chasing a crowd up the main street. They watched in disbelief as an officer shouted an order and the troops opened fire on the people. Seán was relieved that they had not been a part of the shooting of civilians that were already half dead from hunger.

There was no need for them now, so they were sent back to barracks, whilst four companies of the 47th Foot Lancashire regiment arrived to keep order in the town. The ladened ships did not sail from Dungarvan Quay for a few days as the dock workers were afraid of reprisals. The mood in the barracks back in Clonmel was depressing. In the huts there was no music or laughter, just a heavy silence.

The following morning the lieutenant in charge of Seán's platoon told them that he had orders. An assignment with the RIC police was to take place on the Knockmealdown mountains. Arrests of seven tenant farmers were to be made, and the soldiers would assist the police. All the arrests were to be made at the same time, so the platoon and police would be divided into seven groups. After the lieutenant had left, one of the soldiers asked Corporal Phelan why these men were being arrested.

Well now, a few days ago someone tried to kill a landlord who goes under the name of Kiely Ussher. Sure, it all went wrong. After he'd stopped Ussher's coach on a bridge, yer man fired his pistol at him through the coach window. Didn't the gun backfire on himself, and he ran! The landlord was after recognising him, so he was arrested. The whole thing had been plotted by seven of Ussher's tenants. 'Twas them lads that paid the assassin. So, it'll be themselves we'll be arresting tonight.

Another soldier asked,

How did they know it was these seven farmers, and why did they do it?

Seems someone informed on 'em, maybe for money, or to save themselves from being evicted. They plotted because Ussher had been evicting lots of his tenants on the mountainside. The bastard even paid them a pittance to set fire to their own houses Then they were left on the mountainside with nowhere to go and no shelter. Having him shot before the evictions came to them was their plan.

Conor whispered to Billy,

Jaysus, I would shoot him meself!

That evening they went up to the mountain and met up with the RIC. Seven groups of armed police and soldiers then went to the houses of the accused. As Seán's group of twenty marched down a steep dirt track they could see a long white cottage overlooking the valley below. The soldiers surrounded the house while the police entered it with their revolvers drawn. After a few minutes they came out with a young man named Bartholomew Lawton. His hands were tied behind his back and his face was pale. Following behind him was an old woman, his ma, who was crying and holding on to his coat tail. Bartholomew heard one of the policemen as he pulled her away from him say,

Don't worry darlin', we'll be back tomorrow with the bailiffs.

The seven tenants were arrested and taken to the jail in Lismore opposite the castle. A day later, the soldiers were told that the assassin had been tried and sentenced to be hanged. The tenants were to stand trial and would also probably be hanged. (All of the seven tenants were later spared the death penalty. Instead, they were sentenced to hard labour in Bermuda. Only two survived and returned to Ireland. Bartholomew was one of them.)

New orders came the following day, and the relief of the men was tangible. The whole regiment was to be deployed overseas. It was as if all their prayers had been answered. The soldiers were not told the destination only that they were to move out the next morning. That night Seán felt helpless and alone thinking about his family and Niamh. In the morning after the parade, the whole regiment was moved out onto trains. On arriving at the port of Dungarvan they boarded two ships.

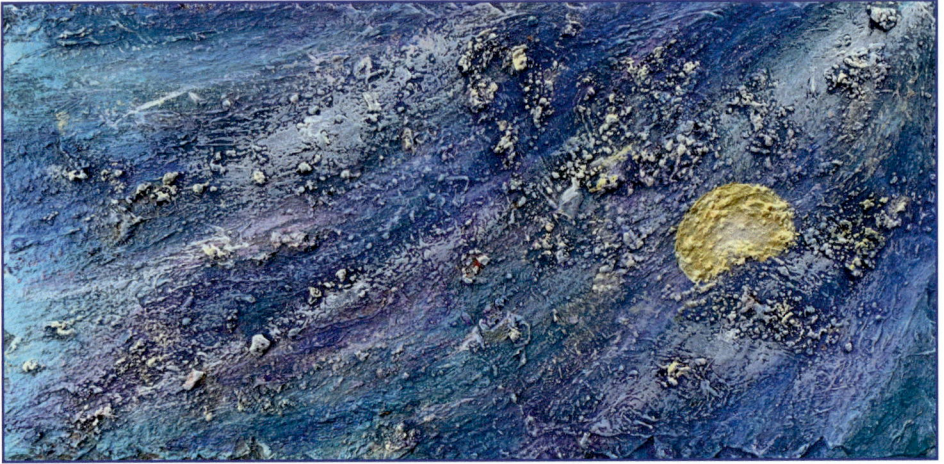

THE LEAVING OF IRELAND

On landing, they travelled from Wales to England where they were taken by train to the east end of London. Marching down dirty streets, the regiment passed dark factories on the way to the East India Docks. Signs of dire poverty and squalor were visible amidst the smoke that drifted down from the tall chimneys. As they marched past the beggars, Seán was thinking that the story of London streets being paved with gold was far from true. After entering the complex of docks, the troops were brought to attention on the quayside. Looming over them were three enormous and beautifully made ships. These ships were EastIndiamen that had been designed and built solely to carry troops.

The new soldiers were overawed by the impossible size of the ships. One of them, the Prince of Wales, was bigger than any ship in the Royal Navy. The East India Company had a greater need because their army numbered 260, 000 which was twice the size of the British Army. Even the docks that the ships were moored in had been built by the company. These troops from Ireland were here to be transported to a war zone, just a cargo in transit that might be described as cannon fodder.

The soldiers began to board the ships and Seán was pleased to see that he and his friends were together and boarding the Prince of Wales. As Seán ascended the gangplank, Conor turned around and said,

Jaysus boy, will ya look at this thing. Ye could fit Sligo town into it and still there'd be room.

Seán smiled back at him but he hadn't really heard him. A thought had just invaded his mind. It almost made him run back down the gangplank and keep running until he found his way home. A certainty had suddenly occurred to him. He would never see Achill Island, his family or Niamh ever again. He felt sick but he did not turn. Instead, he boarded the ship.

Loading was done quickly and efficiently. Feeling bewildered, Seán put down his rifle and kit bag alongside the hammock that he had been allocated. Soldiers were everywhere in the half dark below decks and the noise was deafening. Seán sat in his hammock and retreated into his thoughts. Only now did he fully realise that he no longer had choices or control over his own life.

The voyage was long and monotonous, and the conditions were cramped. However, Seán enjoyed every moment because he loved the sea. It reminded him of home when he would go fishing on the wild sea with his da. This happened during the winter months when the whole population of his village moved from Slievemore to cottages on the coast. During those times they eked out a living by crabbing and fishing. They brought the cows down off the mountain because it was impossible for man or beast to survive the harsh winters up there. Each summer they would return to the mountain pastures with malnourished cows and children. (The settlement lived on the mountain during the summer months. Because of the harsh weather in the winter the whole community would leave the mountain. During the winter they would live by the sea. Through fishing and agriculture they made full use of their environment. The system is known as booleying.)

For Seán, the best time on the ship was in the evening when the decks were empty. Escaping the heat and the relentless noise of the troops below decks was a necessity. On warm and clear nights, with an insatiable wonder, Seán watched the stars, the moon, and the hypnotic swell of the sea. Life on Achill had given Seán an affinity with both sea and mountains.

Standing all alone one night by the ship's rail, Seán noticed something moving on the sea. Amongst the waves he saw a shining ball of golden light. It was the same one that he had seen on the road to Sligo. Once more, he thought of it as a star fallen from the heavens. It was some distance away and moving alongside the ship just above the water. Despite not knowing what this phenomenon was, Seán was aware of a feeling of solace. For what seemed an age, Seán watched until the ball of light disappeared under a wave.

When Seán went below decks he found that Conor and Billy were in conversation with some of the older soldiers. Billy asked Sergeant Murphy where they might be heading to.

Well, tis certain we're heading for India or Burma. Most of us have been out on these East India ships before. Normally it's to India, but recently it's changed to Burma.

Billy asked,

What will we be doing?

It could be anything lad, you might see some fighting. It depends on what part of the country we're sent to. There was a lot of unrest the last time we were in India. We've beaten the Burmese twice now in two wars so that'd be the easiest out of the two.

Some weeks later the troops were summoned on deck. Looking down on them from the poop deck was were major and his officers. The major's briefing was short and to the point.

We are bound for Burma to join our regiment. We have the south and now we have taken Mandalay and the King's palace. In conjunction with the East India company's Indian regiments, we must now establish control in the north. It will not take long before we have the whole country.

With a wry smile he added,

Their king's army has been disbanded, but they continue to fight as rebels. Your main task will be to stamp out this insurrection and eliminate these cowards. We will land in ten days.

Allowing the sergeant-major to dismiss the troops, the major stepped back.

Below decks it became obvious that some of the men had fought in the conflicts that the major had spoken about. Most of the soldiers seemed excited and enthusiastic about going back into action. To Seán and some of the other new soldiers, to hear a British officer talking about eliminating rebels was a cruel irony. It caused an uneasy feeling amongst them. It was a reminder of the fight for freedom that had been waged against British rule for hundreds of years back at home, a fight that was still happening.

Seán could not understand why the other soldiers were so eager to engage in bloodshed. It then occurred to him that they had been soldiers for a long time, and perhaps one day he would be the same. Turning to corporal Phelan, Seán said,

This is madness. Why would you want to be killing people?

Sure, that's the go boy. We have no choice.

Well, I don't want to be part of this. And yerself, why don't you just leave?

The corporal laughed.

You're forgetting yer training lad. Remember, if you so much as disobey an order you'll be flogged. If you or I deserted, they'd find us and finish us with a firing squad. That's why you and I will stay and do as we are told. Remember that, before you have the whip on yer back.

I know, I know, but why are we going there when they already have the war won?

Sure, they have control of the South. I'm guessing, because of the rebels they don't have control of the north. All you have to do boy is follow orders and keep your head down. When we land we'll find out what the craic is and where they're sendin' us.

After a few drinks everyone was speaking Irish because there were no officers around.

After ten more days at sea, they arrived at their destination, the port of Yangon. The Prince of Wales was the first ship to enter the dock, closely followed by the other ships. As they approached the dockside, the soldiers stood to attention on the main deck.

When the ship pulled alongside, Seán could see that the port was busy and chaotic. Soldiers in various uniforms were everywhere amongst the loaded carts. There were even more locals moving around with impossible loads on their heads. Beyond the port was the sprawling city of Yangon. Perched on top of a hill and overlooking the city was an enormous golden temple. This was the Shwedagon Pagoda, the most sacred Buddhist Stupa in Burma. It was the most beautiful thing that Seán had ever seen.

After disembarking, the troops were taken by train to the Royal Irish Regiment headquarters near the banks of the Irrawaddy estuary. Everything they saw and smelled was alien to the new recruits. All of them were overawed and tentative. The widespread barracks were loud and bustling. Putting the newcomers into small groups, an officer allocated them to various wooden huts. Seán, Conor, and Billy stayed together and were put in the same hut with their new section. Inside the hut were 40 other soldiers. Some were lying on their beds, whilst others were playing cards around a big table. All of the soldiers looked over to them. One of them shouted,

Hello lads, come in and have a drink.

They were each handed a bottle of beer and given a chair around the table. Soon they were all chatting. Most of the men in the hut had not been back to Ireland for years. All of them wanted to know how things were back at home. They were worried about their families in this time of the great hunger. The newcomers told them as much as they could about the famine, the clearances and the immigration. As they listened to the stories, the group became subdued, and the mood changed dramatically. In a short while, no-one wanted to talk or hear any more painful news. The room fell silent. To change the subject Seán said,

Would one of youse please tell us what's going on here?

The new recruits began to ask questions about the Burmese wars, the King and the rebels. They wanted to know what a stupa was, and what Buddhism was all about. Seán asked the last question.

Are we going to be fighting soon?

The mood in the room lightened. Aware that the minds of these young soldiers had not yet been corrupted by violence, the older ones smiled at their innocence. It reminded some of them of how they once were.

After a moment one of them said,

Sure, I'll answer your questions lads. I'm the only one here that's been through both wars. My name is Hugh. Will we sit outside so these fellas can carry on with the cards?

Outside the hut, three chaiwallers (slaves) were sitting around a fire boiling a huge cauldron of water. When they saw the soldiers coming out, they got up and started to move away.

Hugh called over to them.

Ah now, there's no need to go, come back. Sure, we'll sit by the fire with you.

Smiling, the chaiwallers returned and sat on the ground, leaving their low wooden stools for the soldiers. Seán sat with them. Hugh said,

These lads come from Bengal in India. They're slaves, only now they call 'em indentured servants. They haven't been home to their families since the beginning of the first war here in Burma. Many of the slaves here are from Bengal. The people there have lived through famine and are poor. Still the East India Company has taxed 'em so much that now they have nothing. You'll see Indian slaves all over the place. In the army they're known as lascars. They're used on the steamers, the railways, construction, and in service. Anyway, I'll tell you what's happened here in Burma.

Years ago, they sent a big army to invade Yangon. They say there were forty thousand troops altogether, most of 'em sepoys and Indian regiments, all belonging to the East India Company. The others were the Queen's soldiers and sailors. The British naval fleet blockaded and bombarded the city until the whole place was on fire. Gunboat diplomacy they call it. It didn't take long; the poor souls didn't stand a chance. By the time the armies went ashore, the whole place was empty. Those that weren't dead or wounded had all left. After drinking and losing their heads the soldiers went on a drunken rampage. They were after setting fire to houses and looting.

God forgive me, but I was there. Jaysus, but it was frightening. Sure, I was only sixteen and just over from Limerick. I was a new recruit like yerselves. I hid in a burnt-out ruin throughout the night. I couldn't believe that people could act in that way. Ah, but I've seen much worse since then. I tell ya, the looting I saw there was terrible, and begod, it was all legal and official. So boys, that was the first war. It was the beginning of the end for Burma.

After two years of occupation, they got a treaty. The armies went back to India and Britain. They left a small force, along with engineers and slaves to build barracks, a railway and a river fleet. Our regiment went back to India to help the East India Company take more territories. For them, it all means more taxes and treasures to take back to England. The golden pagoda - the one you saw when you arrived - they ransacked and vandalised that place. Then, God love us and save us, they turned the temple into a fort. Sure, it's still a fort now. Tis one of the most sacred temples in Burma. Inside are many of their holy relics. God knows what that must have felt like for the Burmese to see it abused like that. It'd be like an army tearing into the Vatican in Rome and desecrating it. Can you imagine how that would be? After that, a lot of the treasures went missing from the temple.

Conor asked,

But didn't they already have the whole of India? What would they be wanting with this country? Haven't they got what they need already?

Greed lad, that's what it is. There are a lot of rich people in England from the Queen down, and this is about making them all even richer. But especially the East India Company. They've gathered more riches than the government. It's also about power. Haven't they already taken plenty of other countries around the world as well. Tis our job to get these places for them.

Billy still could not understand. He asked,

Why did they come back and start another war?

Well, they want to take the rest of the country. After a year, that war has just finished. Now they've all of the South of Burma and a treaty from the King. His troops started to attack British outposts over the last few months despite the treaty. That gave 'em an excuse to finish off the job. My guess is that there is something up there that they really want. So, they needed this excuse to declare war on the King and attack his Palace in Mandalay, the capital. The king had no idea about this and was taken completely by surprise. Jaysus, they weren't pulling any punches. Must have been the shortest war in history, sure it only lasted twenty-two days. They sent three thousand British troops and six thousand Indian troops. There was a whole fleet of steamers and barges with cannons and machine guns. Mandalay is on the river, and the King's defences were along its shore. They blasted those to hell and back. Then they sank the royal steamboat. Before we reached the forts, some of the king's soldiers came out and surrendered. We took 'em prisoner and the King surrendered. They were clever though. We didn't know at the time but most of his army escaped while this was all going on.

Where did they go? asked Seán

They've gone North into the hills and mountains. Since then, they've been led by former officers of King Thibaw's disbanded army. They're attacking all the outposts the Company has built up and they're after using guerrilla warfare. That means they don't play by the rules. Sure, they're rebels to us, but they see 'emselves as the Royal soldiers.

And the King, what about him?

He's been sent into exile in India and the British Government has taken over his palace. Bit by bit they're stripping it of its treasures and sending them back to England as they always do. We watched them taking gold, jewels, silk and ornaments by the boxload, and putting it onto barges. When it gets back to England, it'll all be shared out as gifts for the Royal family, the top brass and Clive, the owner of the East India Company. Over this last year, the East India Company has started exploring the north of Burma. They're taking timber from the forests up there already.

Just then one of the Indian men stood up and gave them all a cup of tea that he had been making while Hugh was talking.

Thank you, Abhoy. Oh, I forgot to introduce you. This is Abhoy and Arup, and that's Benoy - we call him Ben. They are all from Bengal. And then there is Tin Win. He's from Yangon, he was orphaned when we hit the city in the first war. Protestant missionaries came out soon after and set up a school. Tin and many other orphans were taught by them. Teaching was always the job of the Buddhist monks before that, but they left when we took their temple. Tin has been trained to be an interpreter. There are many like him in the barracks.

Tin stood up and spoke across the fire to the newcomers saying,

I am very pleased to meet you gentlemen.

They all replied politely and smiled. Tin's perfect English accent amused them.

After Hugh had introduced the lascars to the new lads, he told them that when there were officers around, they must never show any familiarity with the lascars. He laughed as he added,

Tis a big sin in their eyes.

After chatting for a while, Seán brought the conversation back to the war. Hugh told him,

I think there'll be a big move north soon. Once the north is beaten, they'll control the whole of Burma. It'll be served up as a prize for the Queen, just like India.

So, will we be fighting the rebels?

We will if we can find 'em. It's hard to join 'em in a proper fight. The Burmese ambush and use hit-and-run tactics which are hard to deal with. The British have dealt with this guerrilla warfare in India and South Africa. They win by cutting off any support for the enemy.

What does that mean Hugh? asked Billy.

Because the enemy is hard to find, they break 'em by punishing their villages. Sure, their homes are burned, and their properties stolen or destroyed. Sometimes civilians are shot in firing squads. From what you've told us, it's a bit like what they're doing back home.

Through the flames of the fire Seán noticed that all three of the Indian servants were staring at the ground as Hugh was talking.

Are they ok? They suddenly seem unhappy.

Jaysus, I didn't think. It's because of what I just said. All these three are from the same village and it was burned to the ground by soldiers. After that they were taken away and made slaves of. They've never seen their families since that night. They must have been about your age at the time. So, lads, that's the rule of the British Raj.

Heaven help us, said Seán. I don't think I can be doing this. It's just wrong.

Hugh smiled and said,

But you have no choice, son. Believe me, after a while you'll become used to this life.

Seán's friends nodded in agreement, but Seán knew that he would not. The soldiers went back inside the hut while the lascars slept on the ground by the fire.

For the next fourteen days, all of the troops went through drill, bayonet and firing practice. It seemed that all the soldiers were enthusiastic about the training, which, as always, included the learning of obedience. To survive, Seán pretended to be like the others, whilst protecting his inner self.

One evening, the lieutenant came into the hut and briefed everyone as to what was about to happen.

In two days we will move north. The third battalion will be deployed in Mandalay to support the Indian and British troops that are there already. The second battalion will reinforce the troops of the Punjab Light Infantry and the Royal Welsh Fusiliers. They have just taken Bhamo. Bhamo is a hundred and fifty miles from Mandalay and is the most northerly city on the river. It will become a garrison town. It will enable us to gain control of the mountains and foothills. Our battalion will go to a small outpost two hundred miles north of Bhamo at the base of the hills and mountain ranges. We will be accompanied by three hundred lascars. The outpost is currently manned by British officers and a company of sepoys. The brief is to do reconnaissance of the hills and mountains in order to locate mines and teak forests. Our primary task, however, will be to track down rebels and destroy them. It is also imperative to cut off support from any tribal villages that might be assisting the insurgency. One hundred Siamese mercenaries will be joining us. The Siamese are old enemies of the Kachin people and know the terrain well. That is all. As you were.

Two days later, two troop-carrying steam ships took Battalions 2 and 3 to their destinations. When the ship returned it was made ready for the 1st Battalion to board the following morning.

As the sun was coming up four hundred soldiers marched down to the river, accompanied by three hundred lascars, fifty officers and their horses. The officers boarded the steamship first and went to the upper deck. The soldiers filed onto the main deck and the slaves followed after them. The horses were tied up near the lascars in the aft of the ship.

Keen to see as much as possible on this new adventure Seán, Conor and Billy sat in the bow of the ship. Tin was sitting on the deck nearby as he was there to serve food and drinks to the soldiers in that section.

INVASION

Sitting in a boat on a wide and calm river made Seán happy. On either side of the river, the delta stretched far into the distance. Everything from the vast flat landscape to the palm trees along the shore seemed strange to Seán. Humidity increased as they moved through still waters. Inevitably the loud banter amongst the soldiers gradually became subdued. Complete quiet, humidity and an unchanging landscape all conspired to make Seán feel sleepy. With folded arms resting on the ship's rail, Seán laid his head on them.

Just as he started to fall asleep, he heard movement in the water below. On hearing a splashing sound, Seán opened his eyes. Seven dolphins were swimming and leaping alongside the ship. This reminded him of fishing on the sea with his da. Often, he would watch dolphins chasing the currach. But he had never seen dolphins in a river before. Seán enjoyed watching them racing the ship. Diving one at a time below the surface, the dolphins began to disappear. What Seán did not know was that the dolphins had been expecting him. They were welcoming him into a new world.

Hoping for their return, Seán remained at his viewing point until Billy nudged him.

Look Seán, there's something grand up ahead. I've no idea what it is, I can't make it out.

Seán turned around and saw in the distance a huge mass of golden light blazing in the middle of the river. Holding their breath, the new recruits stared intensely. As the ship neared this vision, the mass of gold came into focus. The middle of the river was a floating temple. Surrounding an enormous dome were tall spires that reached up to the skies. As beautiful as the temple in Yangon, it was even more engaging because of its perfect reflection in the river.

Billy called Tin over and asked him about the temple.

This is called Ye Le Pagoda. It is two thousand years old, and very important for Buddhists.

Seán asked,

Are there many monks here?

No, this temple is empty for the first time since it was built. There are no more monks here. Soon all temples will be the same.

Why is that? There are no signs of any troops here.

Now our king has been sent away there cannot be Buddhists monks. For many years the kings of Burma have always cared for them, like a father looks after his children. I do not think the British Raj will help them. Without the king they cannot live. All the people are not happy.

Seán could hear Tin's sadness in his voice and asked Tin,

Are you a Buddhist?

Smiling, Tin replied,

I have been made a Christian, I am Methodist. I am not allowed to enter any temple. But in my heart, I know that I am Buddhist. One day I shall return to the temples.

Behind them a couple of the soldiers were laughing. One of them, Padraig McBride said,

Don't be after listening to that shite, boy. Sure, we've all heard it before. Buddhists, Muslims, Hindus and Sikhs, they're all just a bunch of heathens.

His friend that was sitting next to him added,

Sure, they're even bigger heathens than the Protestants.

Seán and his friends did not turn around. Calmly, Tin went back to his place as the ship sailed close to the temple.

What Tin had said made Seán see a similarity between the shaping of Tin's religious world and his own. Seán, his family and neighbours were Catholics, but their ancestors were not. The old beliefs had been removed and forbidden. Here in Burma, the changeover to Christianity was just beginning. At home, Christianity had replaced the worship of nature a long time ago. Now the people were controlled by priests and dogma, as well as a foreign master with an alternative form of Christianity.

Seán closed his eyes. He remembered what his da had said as they sat around the fire on the eve of his departure,

Tis good you have the English son from your school, it'll help you get into the army. Before you were born, we had the hedgerow schools. By God, they were good. The teachers would wander the country teaching in the fields. We learnt everything from them, from the old Irish stories to Latin, they taught everything in Irish. Sure, all of it was against the law. Now that the British have allowed Catholic schools, everything ye know must be taught in English. Even speaking Irish is banned in the schools. Sure, it won't be long before everyone in Ireland will be speaking in the foreign tongue.

An hour later they passed the ruins of the defences around Mandalay. Beyond the rubble they could see the king's Palace and smoke rising from the city.

After passing Mandalay, the countryside changed. There were forest-covered hills in the distance and mangrove swamps at the water's edge. Snow-capped mountain ranges were just visible in the far distance. Along the shore were tree-lined fields. Some were being turned over by hand, while others were being ploughed with oxen. Fishermen in canoes cast their nets, and moved slowly along the waterway. Seán was mesmerised as he watched these different aspects of life on the river. Now and then, he would see women washing clothes on bamboo rafts that were tied to the land. There was a constant flow of birds flying up and down the river. Some were familiar to Seán, such as shell ducks and cormorants. Other birds like ibis and storks he had never seen before.

Everything was serene and dream-like as they passed villages of bamboo houses amongst the trees. Interspersed between the villages were white temples and monasteries.

Suddenly, the calm that Seán felt as he watched all of this was dispelled. Men were shouting nearby. Floating towards them was an enormous raft of tree trunks. Standing on the raft were the men that were shouting. Gesturing to the helmsman, they were calling him to move the ship aside. Seeing the raft was an impressive sight. All of the timbers were bound together with rope. Rowers were sitting in a row either side of three tall masts. Seán had never seen anything like this. Pulling alongside the riverbank, the steamer let the floating trees pass. As they passed, the crew of the raft waved and laughed.

Unsure if he was dreaming, Seán turned to Joe and asked,

What in God's name was that?

Joe replied,

They're after just felling those trees. So they can float 'em down river to the docks. Big aren't they? The East India Company have gotten themselves settled in the hills beyond. Sure, they were there even before they took Mandalay. They've found hardwood forests. I'm thinking it's teak. They've been exporting these trees for months from Yangon. Jaysus, those fellas know how to make money.

Seán knew that what they were doing was wrong.

Four days and nights after leaving Mandalay, the steamer arrived at the small harbour of Bahmo. Pulling alongside a bamboo jetty for supplies, they moored for a few hours. When they left that jetty, they had begun the last leg of the river journey. Looking back at the quiet town Seán thought about all the things he had witnessed and experienced on the river. On that steamer he had observed the river people. It seemed that they were completely at one with their environment. He had witnessed a way of living that had been uninterrupted for centuries. His next thought was that he belonged to a force that was about to rip that continuum apart. The lives of these people would never be the same again.

Thoughts of his leaving Slievemore came back to him. Just at that time, his own world was about to be destroyed by clearances and famine. Being on the river somehow brought comfort to him. Along with comfort came an insight. His eyes closed and, in his mind, he saw the people he loved. It was a bright, cold day in Dooagh as Seán looked at a familiar scene. Instinctively he knew that he was observing things that were in the present time. Sitting on the edge of the beach with her two teenage children was Seán's mother. While she was mending fishing nets a few other women nearby were gutting and salting the catch. On the beach, by the enormous crashing waves, Seán's da, Paud was repairing his currach. In the fields behind the women, he saw the cottages. These were the homes the villagers lived in every winter. It concerned Seán to see that most of the houses were empty. There was hardly any sign of life around them. Still, Seán felt much better for seeing his loved ones. Even though he felt happy and relieved, he still had a nagging doubt. He wondered whether Niamh had survived.

Seán's eyes opened and Dooagh vanished. He soon realised that everything around him had changed. The river had narrowed dramatically and there was no longer a shoreline. Instead high cliffs towered some eight hundred feet above them on both sides of the river. Eventually, they passed the cliffs and the river widened. The forest and hills were much closer to the shore than before. They passed another village of bamboo huts on stilts. These were nearer to the water than the other huts Seán had seen. Some of the villagers were outside watching the steamer in silence and suspicion as it went past. This time, there were no smiles or waving. Along the water's edge was a small bamboo raft with a highly decorated shrine tied to it. Looking inside the shrine as they passed it, Seán saw a bronze statue with flowers around its neck. (It was the statue of Shin U Pa Gota, the Saint of all Waters.)

Further up the river, majestic, white pagodas on the hilltops overlooked the forest and river. Later on, he saw, shining between the dark trees, carved white dragons guarding a white monastery. Afterwards, they passed a small temple close to the shore. As they passed it, Seán could smell the subtle fragrances of sandalwood incense and jasmine flowers. Complementing the aromas were the sound of tiny bells tinkling in the wind. All of these added to the calming effect of the river. For a short while, he was no longer aware of the soldiers around him. It was as if he somehow belonged to everything around him.

Suddenly his mind focused when he saw a narrow island ahead in the middle of the river. Stretching for about half a mile, it was filled with thousands of small and simple white domed buildings. They surrounded a much bigger golden temple.

Intrigued, Seán called Tin over and said,

What is this place, Tin?

I do not know. I will ask Abhoy.

Abhoy came over, sat on the deck in front of Seán, and explained.

This island is called ShweKyundaw - in English, the Golden Royal Island. The smaller buildings are shrines called stupas. There are 7,777 stupas here and inside each are relics from Buddha's body. This place is very important to Buddhists.

There was just enough space for the steamer to pass by, and as they did, the smell of incense was once again very strong. Several monks in orange robes were standing by the outer walls. They all nodded towards the vessel as it passed.

The whole island, with its overwhelming and soulful presence, enticed Seán. He wished that he could get off the boat and explore.

After the next day, everything seemed to change once again. The river remained narrow, but the forest receded. The land between the forest and water was no longer fertile. Instead, it was scrubland with no sign of humans or temples. The hills and mountains were much closer, and the only sign of life were the ducks and giant cormorants.

After a cold, humid night the temperature increased rapidly in the morning. Around midday the heat became unbearable. One of the crew who was on watch on the upper deck broke the sleepy silence by calling out,

Jetty ahead, on port side!

As they neared the jetty, Seán saw Indian troops coming out of a bunkhouse. When the ship was tied up, the troops disembarked. They were mustered, and brought to attention, while the lascars unloaded the horses, equipment and supplies. The thirty sepoys from the bunkhouse were also standing to attention with British officers alongside them. Three oxen and carts were waiting to be loaded with the newcomers' supplies and equipment.

Before the soldiers were dismissed, they were told that they would be marching to the outpost at the base of the nearby hills within the next half hour, and that they should fill their billy cans with water from the barrels by the wagons. The lieutenant told the men that it was a march of approximately twenty miles and that they must stay hydrated. Exhausted by the heat, most of the men were lying beneath trees. Seán however wandered over to some structures that were being built by lascars. It looked like they were going to be storehouses, and a supply shop. The shop was nearly complete, and, above its door, flew a flag that Seán had never seen before. Inside was a room full of boxes, and in the middle of them there sat a big man on a chair. Smoking a leaf cigar, the man said,

Hello, son. Can I help ya?

Seán could hardly understand his accent, and replied,

Sure, I was just wondering mister, what's that flag outside?

That's my flag. Tis the flag of Scotland. Laughing, he said,

The English officers don't like me flying it. They say it should be the Union flag, but they have no say over me. My contract's with the East India Company, and me job is to sell supplies.

But surely there's no trade here?

Ah, but there will be soon. Once the company gets its foot in the door, there'll be all kinds of things going through here. The logging has already started and they're talking about taking over mines somewhere in those hills. I'm Andy by the way.

As Andy was talking Seán noticed that there was a fiddle case in the corner. He loved fiddle music and said to Andy,

Is it yerself that owns that fiddle over there? Are you able to play it?

46

Nae lad, I can't play it. I won it in a poker game off some Irish fella. You want it? I'll gladly sell it to ya.

Without thinking, Seán went over and opened the case. After picking up the fiddle and bow, he held it for a while. Somehow it felt familiar. Based on that familiarity, he said yes, even though he could not play a note. Seán had some money and gave it over to Andy. As Seán was Andy's first customer, they shared two small glasses of his best whiskey.

Seán left that empty shop feeling ecstatic. He had the idea that he might be able to teach himself to play. When he got back to the others, he put the fiddle, bow and case inside his knapsack.

Soon they were marching across scrubland that was almost a desert. Ahead of the troops were the officers on their fine horses. Behind the troops were the sepoys. Following them were the slaves carrying anything that could not have been loaded onto the carts. There was no hope of shade in that vast, open space, and the heat was relentless.

It was late afternoon when they arrived at a small town nestled at the foot of a wooded hillside. The houses in the town looked just like the ones along the river. On the edge of the town were new wooden buildings that looked like those back at the barracks. There were more huts still being built. The troops and lascars were told that they would be staying under canvas. The officers were to stay in one of the new buildings. A hundred sepoys occupied the bamboo huts in the town. The original inhabitants of those huts had been forced out.

Over dinner that evening the officers met Mr. Sanders, the East India company's representative. He told them that his role was to oversee the development of the outpost. He said that he wanted to explain to the officers what they might expect, and what the East India Company hoped to achieve. The officers felt uncomfortable, as they were not used to taking advice or orders from civilians.

Sanders began.

These hills and mountains are unknown to us. It's important that we learn where things that are of interest to us are located. We have already discovered acres of teak forest, so we assume there will be more. In the king's palace was found an abundance of gold, diamonds and rubies. Locals have informed us that the source of this wealth lies within these hills.

It is hoped that, in your travels, you will discover these mines.

Developing this area cannot take place while there are rebels running around, and villages that protect them. We need you to solve this problem. Because this area is so vast and unknown to us, we have enlisted a band of Siamese mercenaries. They know these hills very well, and will assist you. Siamese have been raiding villages and temples here for centuries. They will be your guides. This particular band is known to be experienced and to contain ruthless warriors. The headman also speaks English, so they are perfect for the job.

The lieutenant asked,

When will they arrive?

They are travelling up the river, and will arrive tomorrow morning.

In the morning, the whole camp came to a standstill when they saw the one hundred Siamese mercenaries. In the distance they were walking through the heat haze towards the base. When they came into focus, they were a formidable sight. Each carried an enormous sword and a rifle. Somchai, the headman, was greeted by the lieutenant and taken to the officers' quarters. The rest were shown to their tents and not seen till the next morning.

The lieutenant told Somchai that he wanted to discuss the plan of action. In effect, it was a conversation to find out what either side had to offer. When the lieutenant explained that their purpose was to seek out and kill as many rebels in the Kachin hills as possible, Somchai smiled for the first time.

This is good for us. Kachin people are our enemies, and we know them well. I take you to many villages where there will be warriors. Some will be from the King's army but most of those will be away raiding your troops and outposts.

Exactly and this is an exercise to teach these people a lesson, so we will destroy their homes and kill any armed men we find, be they rebels or not. They must learn that we are their new masters.

This is good. There is something I want to tell you. It is about a temple in the mountains that was raided three hundred years ago by our people. It was not a Buddhist temple, because in these hills they worship the gods of nature. Our elders tell us that there was great wealth in this temple. There were a hundred priests, and a hundred temple cats. In the raid, they killed the head priest. Before they could kill the rest of them, a Kachin army attacked them. Some got away with gold and jade, but they left behind much more. Since then, we have never found this temple. Perhaps this time we will find it. If we do, then your men will guard the temple and we will kill the priests. After that we divide the treasure between you and me. You put your share on a ship back to England. We will be rich.

The lieutenant smiled and agreed that it was a good idea. He was being diplomatic as he believed that the story was unlikely. He also did not trust Somchai.

The following morning the whole camp prepared for the move into the hills. The regiment was divided into two platoons with equal numbers of mercenaries between them. Platoon A was to go straight into the hills and travel east. Seán's Platoon B was to travel North. Somchai said that after about a ten-mile journey along the plains, Platoon B will turn into the hills and travel North.

Soon after they had started marching, Seán looked up into the sky to see a dark bird flying high above them. It transpired that the bird accompanied them throughout the march. Marching along the plains without shelter from the sun was gruelling. Some relief came when they finally turned into the tree-covered hills. From that point, Seán could no longer see the bird in the sky.

As they climbed a steep hill Seán looked back across the line of soldiers. Below were the lascars and a line of mules carrying the equipment and supplies. He felt sorry for them. Later the platoon stopped for a rest and water.

The lieutenant addressed the men.

By nightfall we shall arrive at a village. Some of the Siamese troops are going ahead of us and will surround the village. They will wait there until we arrive. The rest of the Siamese are scouting the area and guiding us.

As the soldiers rested, some of the lascars brought around pieces of bread and water. Tin came to Seán, Conor and Billy with their rations. He squatted down and, as he passed the food to them, Tin whispered,

I am going to run away when we get to the village. My friends have told me that they have seen what we are going to do before. They say that the men in the village will be shot, and the houses will be burned. This will carry on in every village that we go to. These are my people. I cannot be part of this, and I will not be a slave anymore. I know this will be hard for you as well, so maybe you come with me?

Tin got up quickly and carried on delivering the rations to the other soldiers.

Seán, Conor and Billy were shocked at what Tin had told them. He was right. None of them could willingly inflict violence on innocent civilians. They wondered how they could possibly join Tin.

All three sipped their water, and stared at the sun setting over the parched lands and river below. None of them had ever seen such a violent sky. Even the Irrawaddy was a blood red, and the sun's bright reflection hovered in the centre of it. Circling high above the sun's reflection was that dark bird that had followed them. In that light Seán could see that the bird was a raven.

Seán's mind emptied. For a few minutes he left his body and became a part of that red sky and river. He heard a heartbeat and returned to his own inner self. He turned around to look past the resting soldiers, to see at the edge of a nearby oak forest, the white deer he had seen on the road to Sligo. At first, the deer was grazing but then she raised her head and looked at Seán. All the while, the sound of her heartbeat continued. The deer walked carefully between the soldiers that were lying and sitting down. They seemed to be unaware of her. Once past the soldiers, she ran to the top of the hill and then out of sight. Seán knew that he was getting closer to Brigid.

Soon after, the march continued. In the twilight, the temperature began to drop. Eventually they reached the outskirts of the village. Conor, Billy and Seán were in section one. They were to advance into the village, while the others stayed back. As they approached the village, they could see the light of a fire. The lieutenant blew a whistle and the hidden Siamese started to walk into the village from the other end. They had their swords drawn and the Irish soldiers had their rifles at the ready.

When they entered the village, it soon became clear that there was no sign of life, not even barking dogs. There was a large fire in the centre of the village. Above the fire was a cauldron, full of boiling water.

All the soldiers came to a halt and were brought to attention. Comchai looked angry and shouted out for all of the villagers to come out of their houses. Nothing happened, there was just silence. Lieutenant Williams shouted for all of the lascars to come up with the paraffin torches, and told section one to keep their guns trained on the houses.

Billy, Seán and Conor were afraid of what might happen. They were holding their rifles like the others, ready to shoot. When the lascars arrived, they were ordered to leave the torches by the fire and search all the houses. They were told to bring out people, weapons and food.

Eventually the lascars came out with nothing. The lieutenant was angry and shouted at them as if it was their fault. Comchoi said to him quietly,

We must search the area quickly. The cauldron is boiling, they cannot be far. We must find them before they warn the next village.

The lieutenant ordered Corporal Phelan to take ten troops and ten lascars and set fire to the houses, and then to join them further along the path when they had finished. He ordered the Siamese to move forward into the woods. The soldiers were to stay on the path leading out of the village. He told Comchai to send a messenger if they found the villagers.

On leaving the village, the troops and lascars searched the woods bordering the path as they moved forward. Dense undergrowth made the woods almost impenetrable and their progress very slow. Each small group had a lantern between them. The task seemed impossible. There were two other soldiers and two lascars in Seán's group. One of the lascars was Benoy.

Meanwhile in the village the corporal briefed the men.

This needs to be done quickly so we can catch up with the others. Set fire to the inside of the houses then come out and light the roofs. Four men to each house.

Billy and Conor were in one group with Tin and Arup. As they stood by the fire, lighting their torches, Billy said,

Jaysus, I watched the bastards burn down my home. I'll not be doing this. I'm telling Phelan to stick this torch up his backside.

Tin whispered,

Billy, I am going to escape now. You and Conor come with me. First, we set fire to one house, but we will never do it again. Will you come with me?

I will, said Billy, and then he looked at Conor, who added, Of course!

Tin spoke quickly.

When we searched the houses, I found a door at the back of the third house that has a path outside. We must go in that house now and burn it. Then we go out back door. Arup must stay and he will go to front and set roof on fire.

Conor said,

Will you not be coming with us Arup?

I cannot, I have family in India. If I desert, they will be punished.

There was no time to talk anymore. All four of them ran to the third house. When they got inside, they could see the opening with material hanging down over it. After setting everything alight, they rushed out through the opening. The flames were close behind them. Running down the dirt track into the forest, they escaped the fires and the madness.

While they were escaping, Arup ran out of the front door and set fire to the roof. He then joined the rest of the men as they ran through what was already an inferno. After regrouping they marched at speed along the forest path. Nobody noticed that three of their group were missing.

ANOTHER STEP

Flames appeared above the trees turning the night sky red. Troops and lascars that had gone ahead stopped to watch. Those flames, and the sound of the houses burning, invoked vivid memories for many.

Unaware of his friends' escape, Seán wondered if Billy's temper had gotten him into trouble.

When Seán turned back to start hacking at the undergrowth he heard that heartbeat again. Deep in the forest, the white deer was watching him. Knowing exactly what he must do, Seán turned to Benoy,

Benoy, I must leave. I'll not see you ever again my friend. I hope you find your freedom one day.

Benoy understood what was happening and felt both happy and sad.

It's not possible to get through this forest, but I know you will find a way. Yes, I will have my life back one day, Seán. Khoda Hafez (Goodbye).

When Seán took a step towards the deer, a clear path appeared ahead of him. With his pack and rifle on his back, he moved cautiously. Standing high up in the dark forest, the deer shone like a lighthouse guiding a lost ship.

The deer started moving away, so Seán began to move faster. Turning around to see if he was being followed, Seán saw only tangled undergrowth. The path behind him had gone. Although unable to see the troops, Seán could still hear their voices. He knew at that point that he had left their world.

As he got deeper into the forest, the path steepened. To Seán's dismay, the deer disappeared just as a full moon came out from behind a cloud. With the new source of light, Seán carried on, hoping to see the deer again.

Along the path he found a small clearing and stopped to rest. Soon after he had closed his eyes, something moved in a nearby tree. Looking up he saw a raven on a branch above him. The bird was watching him. Slowly he stood up. Both Seán and the bird kept perfectly still, whilst looking at each other. Even though Seán thought it was impossible, he wondered if this was his old friend. When the bird tilted its head on one side, he knew it was his own Cormac.

Seán heard a voice in his mind. It was a response to his thoughts.

Yes, I am Cormac. And yes, we are now able to talk to each other. Áine was right, the Aos Sí chose you to find me beneath the hawthorn tree.

Even though Seán was amazed to hear Cormac's voice he still interrupted,

But why, why did they choose me?

They chose you because of your ancestors. Finding me was arranged so that we can be together throughout your odyssey. The path you just stepped onto has brought you closer to the next part of your learning. You have also stepped closer to the other side, so many things will now become possible. To help you in your quest, Brigid has given you the gift of understanding. This means you are now able to understand and speak in the languages of all creatures and humans.

Wide-eyed and overwhelmed, all that Seán could say was,

Ah jaysus, that's grand.

This is just the beginning. You must rest, take out your bed roll and sleep. In the morning you will climb the mountain.

Before you go, can you tell me one thing? What has happened to Conor, Billy and Tin? I'm worried about 'em.

I watched your friends as the village was set alight. You will learn what has happened to them when you sleep.

After Cormac had flown off, Seán went to sleep and started to dream. He watched Conor, Billy and Tin escape from the burning village. Then Seán woke up, relieved and ready to take on his new challenges. Standing close to him on the ground was Cormac.

You must start now. The path gets steeper and your climb will get harder.

Cormac flew off.

With his pack and rifle on his back, Seán started to walk up to the foot of the mountain. Despite the gruelling journey on that steep path, Seán arrived at the bottom of the mountain face. Initially the climb was easy for Seán, despite the heat. Fewer places for his feet to find a purchase made the climb more difficult. Following hours of slow climbing, he found himself below what seemed to be a ledge. Reaching up, he pulled himself on to the ledge. Exhausted, he laid on his back and looked up at the cloudless sky.

When he rolled over, he was shocked. In front of him on a small, grassy plateau were people and animals. Most of the people were sitting along the bank of a turquoise pool, under the shade of stunted oak trees. Plunging into the pool was a waterfall cascading down the mountainside. The trees hung over the water with highly scented flowers growing beneath. It seemed like a small paradise.

All of the people were looking at Seán and smiling. It surprised Seán that they seemed so friendly despite him bearing a rifle and wearing the uniform of their enemy. He was not sure what he should do next.

An upright and elderly man with a white beard walked over to Seán. After bowing his head, he said,

Welcome Seán. I am Yue, the headman and shaman of our village. Come and join us by the water.

Seán knew that the old man was speaking a foreign language (which was Jingpho), yet he understood every word. He was also relieved that someone had taken the initiative to talk to him. The old man led Seán to a gap between the people at the water's edge. Children swam in the pool, and the flower-scented air was full of their laughter. Wandering freely amongst the people were chickens, goats, dogs and ponies. Seán was enchanted by these people who gave him food and drink as he sat amongst them.

Sitting between Yue and a statuesque eagle, Seán thought that everything seemed impossible. Turning to Yue he asked,

Where have you all come from? How would ye be getting here?

The village that the soldiers burned was our home. Before the soldiers arrived, we came here to the temple for safety.

How did you know the troops were coming?

Nodding towards the eagle, Yue said,

This is Nay, the protector of the temple and all the villages around this mountain. She told us they were coming, and to leave our village.

Confused, Seán asked,

Can you and Nay speak to each other?

For generations our people have lived with these eagles. We have learnt to understand them. As a shaman, I can communicate with them. Every village has a shaman. Nay is warning the neighbouring villages of the danger that is coming. When the soldiers get to the villages, the people and food will be gone. There will be nothing for them to take. With no food, the soldiers will have to leave the hills or starve.

But your homes, they have all gone. What will you do?

We will stay here in the temple until the troops have gone. We will return and build new houses. Every village has homes in other places. We move around because we grow crops in different climates and at different times of the year.

Seán was intrigued.

Sounds like our life on Achill. What crops do you grow?

We grow rice on the side of the hills. We change where it's grown each year. Higher up the mountain we grow potatoes, just like your people do. Nowhere else in Burma are potatoes grown because it is too hot.

How do you know that we grow potatoes back home?

We know a lot about your country, and you as well. Ever since you started to follow the golden ball of light, we have been waiting for you. Nay told me to expect you, as you were with the soldiers.

Seeing Seán looking puzzled, Yue said,

Soon you will understand.

Then, to Seán's surprise, Cormac flew down and landed near him. Speaking into his mind Cormac said,

Look up into the trees, Seán.

In the trees all around the pool were all kinds of exotic birds. Suddenly, all the birds left the trees and circled above the lake. This created a moving sheet of translucent colour. In places, the display was punctuated by the backdrop of dark oak leaves. Hundreds of giant butterflies joined them. They circled beneath the birds to create another translucent layer. Shining through vivid wings, the sun transferred all the colour to the surface of the pond.

Spellbound and enchanted, Seán stared at the birds, butterflies and moving colours in the pool. In disbelief he asked Yue,

Tis mad. Is it a dream I'm having?

No, this is real. They are here to greet you.

I don't understand ...

It is time to go into the temple, Seán. There your questions will be answered.

Getting up slowly, the old man called out above the birdsong. Everybody started to move. As the children left the pond, some adults gathered belongings. The others started to load up the ponies. The children from the pond rounded up the dogs, chickens and goats. Along with the ponies, they all formed a line at the base of the rock face.

Yue led the people to a copse that bordered the plateau. After following the people to the trees, the butterflies and birds hovered above them. When they reached the trees, they stopped in front of a wall of ivy. It seemed impassable. Leaving the line, a few men came forward and grabbed the ivy. Together, they pulled it aside, as if they were opening a curtain. It revealed an entrance to a tree lined avenue. The branches of the trees arched over a stone path to touch the mountainside. Shining through red and yellow leaves, dappled sunlight made the avenue vibrant. Together the butterflies and birds flew through the opening. The birds landed in the trees further down the pathway. Following them were the butterflies, but instead of landing they danced below the birds. Slowly, the procession followed. On reaching the butterflies and birds, Yue stopped. He placed his hand on the mountainside and all the butterflies flew over. They landed in a cluster of colour, just above his hand.

Yue said to Seán,

We have reached the Temple.

The entire entourage, including the animals, became quiet. Even the birds were silent. As Yue removed his hand from the stone, there appeared two enormous doors set into the mountain wall. Everyone cheered and the general noise returned.

Yue turned to Seán saying,

These doors are ancient, look at them a while before you knock.

Detailed carvings of animals and birds were moving all over the oak door. Wide-eyed Seán watched in disbelief. Quietly, Yue said to him,

You must knock once on the door.

Grabbing hold of the enormous brass knocker, Seán hit the door. The knock made the whole mountain reverberate. Watching the door slowly opening, Seán stepped back to stand next to Yue. In the doorway stood a tall man with outstretched arms.

It is good to see you, Yue. Hello Seán, welcome to the temple. In Ireland my name is Abhean. Here I am called Denpo. Come in, and please leave your rifle by the door.

Of course.

Seán and Yue went inside. Standing on a walkway, a gallery that had been carved from the mountain, they looked down at the temple interior. Suspended below a domed ceiling, the walkway circled high above the enormous cavern. Seán stared at the vast empty room with a blue slate floor. There were no windows, yet the room was full of daylight. Yue signalled for the others to enter. A procession of animals and people filed in slowly through the big doors. It was familiar to them, and they quietly moved along the gallery.

Yue said,

I will leave you now and go with my people to take the animals to the fields. Denpo will go with you.

Guiding their animals, the families went along the gallery. An opening gave them access to a path leading down to the pastures.

As Seán and Abhean descended the staircase, Seán marvelled at the size of the room. Looking up to the ceiling he saw intricate carvings of wild cats, deer, and elephants. A broad shaft of sunlight shone down from the chimney. There was a perfect circle of sunshine on the floor. Seán was surprised to see, shining brightly within it, the golden ball. When they reached the bottom of the stairs, Seán asked Abhean,

Can you see the golden ball?

Yes, I can Seán, it's beautiful. Step down onto the slate and close your eyes, just for a moment, and then open them.

Seán did as Abhean had asked. When he opened his eyes, he was shocked once more. The golden ball had been replaced by his other travel companion, the white deer. Standing perfectly still with unblinking eyes, she captured Seán in her stare.

Without moving, he whispered to Abheen,

Ah Jaysus, will ye look at herself. Will we go over?

Abhean smiled and replied,

No, close your eyes just once more, and then open them.

Seán did what he was asked. When he opened his eyes, the deer had gone. Instead, he saw a tall woman standing in the beam of light. Seán thought that this beautiful and etherial being must be an angel. Her pale, luminous skin contrasted with her hair which was the colour of fire. There was a boldness in her topaz eyes. Complementing all of this was her long dress that was the colour of a summer sky.

Smiling at Seán, she stepped out of the sunlight into the shadowy room. Without the sun's rays, the fiery colour in her hair became golden. Her eyes changed to the colour of her dress. Speaking in a soft voice she said,

I am the golden ball, and also the white deer that travelled alongside you. I am a spirit of nature, but in your world I take on human form. In Ireland my name is Brigid. Here, people call me Tsun.

Speechless and transfixed, Seán stared at her as she walked over to him. Taking hold of his hand she said,

In your young life you have learnt much. Now, you will learn far more. First in this temple, and then on your travels.

Letting go of Seán's hand, Brigid disappeared. Abhean said,

You will see her again soon, Seán. Let us join the others outside.

Walking down a long corridor towards daylight Seán tried to comprehend what he had just witnessed. He asked,

What would be the name of this place? I've never seen anything like it.

It is known as Lao Tsun, which means the temple of Tsun. Here in Burma, Brigid's name is Tsun Kyan-Kse. In English it means the Goddess of Transmigration.

Seán was confused. Abheen smiled and said,

One day you will understand.

After passing many doorways, Abhean stopped and opened one of them.

Leave your bag here, Seán, this is your room. At times you will need solitude.

Inside the room was a stool, and blankets on the floor. Placing his pack on the stool, Seán removed the fiddle case and took out the fiddle.

Abhean smiled and said,

You have an ancient fiddle there Seán. I am glad that you bought it.

Seán was surprised,

How do you know?

The Tuatha De Danann wanted you to have it. But you had to choose it for yourself, so they arranged it.

That's grand. I'm glad they sent it my way.

Knowing that he would be told the reasons soon, Seán did not ask any more questions.

Carrying on down the hall, they came out into a garden. Standing in the doorway, Seán looked across the garden to see a valley surrounded by snow-capped mountains. Within the valley were meadows, woodlands, and fields. Many people were in the garden harvesting vegetables, flowers, and fruit. Amongst the harvesters he recognised some of the villagers. In the nearest meadow he could see children playing, accompanied by chickens, goats, and cats.

Abhean said,

Everyone spends their days out here in the valley so they can work in the sun's warmth.

Smiling Seán said,

Sure it'd be the same at home. We'd be always outside. Our house was just for the sleeping and cooking. Oh, and milking the auld cow in the bad weather.

They walked around the gardens and Seán listened to the people singing in harmony. When they went into the meadows, Seán noticed children stroking a white horse. He had never seen such a magnificent creature. On an impulse, Seán ran over and started to stroke the horse's nose. One of the children said to him,

His name is Star and he's here for you Seán.

Seán laughed and said, Ah go on now, why would ya say that?

Abhean arrived at that moment and said,

Because it's true Seán, he is to be your companion, and will be a part of your journey.

All six children stood smiling at Seán because he was so lucky to have such a present.

Star talked into Seán's mind.

I have only just arrived in this valley, and I have been asked to help you in your quest.

I don't understand.

There are places that are important to your learning. I will take you to them, and we will share our new freedom.

At home I'd be often riding bareback on the plough horse along the beach. That was no problem at all. But to be riding a thoroughbred like yerself would be beyond me.

Tomorrow, I will show you how we can ride together as one. The sun is setting and Abhean is waiting to take you back to the garden. In the morning we shall ride across these meadows as one.

Once again Seán was overwhelmed. The course of events had developed so quickly, in such an unimaginable way. In the garden, everyone was sitting on the ground and eating. There seemed to be twice as many people now. Sitting next to many of them were the light-coloured cats that he had seen in the fields. Seán was given a plate of vegetables, fruit and rice. He and Abhean sat with the others.

Seán asked,

Are you not eating Abhean?

He smiled. I am a spirit, Seán. I do not eat.

As people finished their meal they began to enter the passageway to the temple. Seán and Abhean followed them. Only the people with the cats remained seated. As they walked down the passage, Abhean said,

In your room there are some new clothes for you to wear. Would you mind bringing your uniform down to the hall? Perhaps you could also bring your fiddle. Seán said that he would be happy to. After changing into his new Burmese clothes, he brought his fiddle, bow and uniform out of the room. When they entered the great hall, Seán noticed how different it looked. All around the walls were flaming torches. Moonlight had replaced the sunlight. It shone from the opening onto a blazing fire. Shadows from the moonlight and fire danced over the walls and the faces of the families sitting on the floor. Amongst the people, Seán noticed some strange-looking instruments. Paintings of mountainous landscapes amidst huge swathes of abstract colour covered the walls.

Abhean asked Seán to follow him to a stone podium. It was carved into the wall and faced the hall.

Your hosts are waiting for you, Seán. Leave your uniform by the steps and go on up. I shall follow.

When Seán stepped onto the podium with his bow and fiddle, he saw Brigid. Dressed in Burmese clothes she sat on a stone bench with three other people. Smiling at Seán, Brigid asked,

Did you enjoy your time in the valley?

Oh, I did, I did. What a grand place and a fine horse. Sure, I loved it all.

Brigid smiled.

Please, sit beside me so I may introduce you to my friends and my son. We all belong to the Tuatha Dé Danann.

Seán sat down and looked at the serene faces of the tall people.

This is my son, Creidhne. In the human stories of my sons, there are three gods of the arts known as Tri Dée Dána. Creidhne works in gold, brass, bronze, and stone. He also paints.

Stories of the Tri Dee Dána were a part of Seán's childhood memories and now he was speechless.

Leaning forward, Creidhne said,

I am honoured to meet you Seán. We have all followed the journey that has brought you here.

Curious, Seán asked,

Was it yerself that did the paintings and carvings around the hall? Oh, and the door with the moving animals on?

All but the paintings. Abhean did those.

Brigid continued her introductions. This is Caer Ibormeith. In the stories she is a princess that has been cursed to spend every second year of her life as a swan. But really she changes into a swan whenever she pleases. Water is her link to the other world.

Caer did not speak. Smiling, she bowed her head like a swan. With green eyes, white skin, and long white hair, she was the palest of the spirits.

Brigid continued.

Finally, this is Cana Cludhmor. In this world she is known as the Goddess of music, inspiration, and dreams. With golden strings made from her own golden hair, she created the first harp.

Seán could see that next to Cana was a harp. Seán had never seen one, but he had heard of them. Cana and the harp were as beautiful as each other. Somehow, she made him feel that he had entered a dream.

In a soft voice Cana spoke to him,

I am looking forward to hearing this fiddle once again, Seán. I can remember its exquisite sound, and how wild it could be at times.

How do you know of this fiddle?

Dermot, your ancestor would play it at every hooley. We all loved his music. This fiddle holds his spirit, and it has passed down through many musicians. You are its natural heir and now it is yours.

Brigid spoke.

Finally, Abhean who you have already met. He is a storyteller, a poet, and an artist.

To Seán, Abhean already seemed like an old friend.

Nodding towards the floor below, Brigid said,

Look Seán, now the monks are coming in to join the others.

A line of men and women dressed in black robes entered the hall. Seán had already seen most of them outside. There was a cat walking alongside each one of the monks' bare feet. All of the cats were small, with cream-coloured fur. Their faces, ears, and tails were grey. The monks and cats sat on the floor with the villagers. This took a while because there were a hundred monks and a hundred cats. When they were all seated, the hall became silent.

Knowing Seán was intrigued Brigid said,

Before you ask Seán, you will find out about the monks tomorrow. Tonight, we are going to celebrate your first step closer to our world. I would like you to do something to start those celebrations.

Of course, replied Seán. What is it?

Your rifle, uniform, and the riding tackle that belonged to Star are the remnants of both of your recent past. They are the last material things that connect you to that part of your lives. Throw it all on the fire, Seán, and the flames will turn them to ash. Everything is waiting for you. Go now and be rid of them. Star is waiting for you.

To Seán's surprise, Star was looking up at him from the floor below. Seán and Star made their way along a gap between the seated people towards the fire. Watching them, the people and cats remained seated. Throwing his uniform and Star's tack, one piece at a time, into the blazing fire gave Seán great pleasure. The last thing was his rifle. When he had finished, everyone stood up and cheered. Finally, Seán and Star were no longer connected to their military past. Musicians in the crowd started to play instruments that Seán had never seen before. Beneath the melodic music, Star went back outside through the passageway.

Seán returned to the podium and his new friends. The temple came alive with music and dancing. Sensibly, the cats watched from stone seats along the walls with complete indifference. Many instruments were being played. It was a vibrant sound that he instantly fell in love with.

Laughing for the first time in ages, Seán said to Brigid,

I've never heard music like this before, tis grand. Look, even the wains are dancing.

Brigid was also laughing.

It is wonderful, Seán, and it's only just begun. Once things like this, with fires and dancing, happened all over Ireland on feast days like Lughnasa. That was before the Christians came with all the changes that followed in their wake.

When the music and dancing stopped everyone went back to sitting on the floor. The cats scurried over to the monks and sat with them. The people were lively and noisy, but that changed when Cana stood up. Not a sound could be heard as she walked over to her harp in the centre of the stage. Sitting down at the harp, Cana began to play. From the very first note, the music carried a pulse through the air that was felt by everyone. Like the audience, Seán was captivated. Although the lament she played sounded Irish, Seán did not know it.

After a few minutes, Abhean stood up. Taking hold of Seán's fiddle and bow, he walked over to Cana. With closed eyes he effortlessly accompanied her lament. The combined sound of the fiddle and the harp tore into the hearts of every living being there. Instinctively, Seán knew that this music was related to the sad times of his own country, as well as Burma and many other lands. Seán had never heard such emotive fiddle playing. It complemented Cana's golden harp perfectly. When the music came to an end, the temple was completely still and silent. It was as if a spell had been cast.

Abhean came over to Seán and held the fiddle out towards him,

It is your turn to play Seán.

Ah no, sure, I can't play at all.

Brigid looked at Seán and said,

Draw the bow across the fiddle and think of your favourite tune. I know you can do this.

Reluctantly, Seán stood up and went over to the centre of the stage. Cana had gone back to her seat and the Harp had disappeared. The hall was still quiet. Only the shadows from the fire were dancing now. Knowing everyone was watching with an expectation that he could not meet, Seán felt foolish. He thought of his favourite tune. It was the one his uncle had played on the night before he left. He did not know its name, only that it was by O'Carolan. In those few moments prior to when he lifted the fiddle to his chin, he had every single note of that tune in his mind. Closing his eyes, Seán began to play. As his bow touched the strings, Seán's hands began to work a miracle. The reel had started. Echoing loudly around the hall, the music instantly animated his audience. There were shouts amongst the crowd that were like the calls he would have heard at home. Enjoying every moment, Seán played flawlessly.

When he finally opened his eyes, the room had changed. The central shaft of light had spread, and moonlight now filled the room. The paintings on the walls became clearer. Both the abstract and figurative images were moving around the walls. All the birds from the gallery were flying around the ceiling with the eagles. Cormac was amongst them. In the ceiling, the carved animals had become animated by the music. They were following each other in a continual and lively procession around the inner dome.

Seán had another surprise when he looked down. The audience were on their feet and dancing in sets. Even the children at the back were in full swing. Seán could not believe it. It was as if he was in a ceilidh back at home. As he played, he went effortlessly from the reel to a jig, and so did the dancers. The pure, natural power that he felt in that music was something he had never known before.

Looking around the temple once more, he saw that the paintings on the walls had changed. Now the abstract paintings had become fields, hills, and mountains. To his surprise, the spirits he had been sitting next to were now dancing. Noticing the paintings once more, he realised that one of the painted landscapes was of Dooagh, the fishing village that was his home in the winter months. Further around the walls he saw his beloved mountain, Slievemore. As he watched, the imagery transformed into his summer village and his home. Seeing that it was summer in the painting confused him, because there was no sign of life. His village was empty, and there were no cows in the fields above. As he looked for signs of life, the wall paintings changed into a calm sea. It encircled the whole dance floor. Seeing those glimpses of his old life inspired him to play tunes that he had never heard before. Without realising it, he was composing new pieces from within.

After playing for nearly an hour, Seán stopped. The shouts and clapping lasted for a long time. Brigid, the other spirits, and Seán returned to their stone seats. Breathless, the people below sat back down on the floor. The wall art and the stone carvings became still once more.

Brigid stood up and spoke,

Thank you, all, for celebrating the beginning of Seán's new life with us. Thank you, Seán, for such an amazing performance. Tomorrow Seán will begin his learning. Goodnight everyone.

All the people and the cats returned to their rooms. Abhean said to Seán with a smile,

You played that beautiful fiddle so well - and after you saying that you couldn't play!

Sure, I couldn't, how did that happen?

Brigid put her hand on his shoulder.

Now you have the understanding of music as well as language. These are gifts that will be helpful to you.

I must ask you, Brigid, how in heaven's name do all these people know the Irish dancing?

We have taught them for many years about the history of Ireland. Because they love music and dance so much, we also taught them Irish dancing and music. As you can see, they are very good at it.

Oh, they are, they really are.

Goodnight now, Seán.

After she had spoken, Brigid and the other spirits disappeared. As the last of the people and cats left, the flames died, and the hall became dark.

In the morning, Seán went outside to join everybody in the garden. They were all getting ready to swim in the river that fed the waterfall. Soon Seán was swimming with them in warm water the colour of peat. Along the river were shallow inlets and sandy beaches that the children played in. Mothers knelt in the shadows of overhanging trees and bathed their babies. In the middle of the river, people swam amongst ducks and geese. Moving slowly amongst them was a white swan. Seán felt pleased to be swimming once more.

One of the monks came down to the river to tell the bathers that it was time to eat. Everyone except Seán got out of the river and prepared to move down to the garden. In the new tranquillity he decided to stay a little longer with the river birds.

After a short swim he sat on the riverbank. Leaving the other birds, the swan came towards Seán and swam in the shallow waters. To Seán's surprise she spoke into his mind,

It is me Seán, Caer. It is time for me to leave and I wanted to tell you that I am proud of you. In all of your journeys know that I will always be near you. In one of your lives, I shall be a messenger. Goodbye for now, Seán.

Caer turned around, swam up-river and took flight.

Seán was intrigued by the idea that she would one day deliver a message to him. Standing up, he walked quickly to catch up with the others. The slow procession of wet people going down to the garden amused Seán. Nobody bothered to dry themselves because the hot sun dried them naturally as they walked and sang together.

It occurred to Seán that these people were simply joyous about every aspect of life, of just being alive. Moving through the orchard, everyone picked some fruit. On arriving in the gardens, they sat on the grass. Bowls of rice were followed by the fruit they had picked.

As Seán finished eating, Brigid appeared.

I would like to talk to you Seán. Shall we walk back to the river so we may be alone?

After walking to the river in silence, they sat down on a rock overlooking the water. Speckled trout swam in the river as the purple dragonflies played amongst the reeds. Gently rippling water was the only sound. Without looking at Seán, Brigid smiled and said,

Before we start, I want to know if you have questions about anything at all.

Without hesitation, Seán replied,

Oh, dear God, I really want to know about my family and Niamh. Are they still alive and safe? When I saw the cottages on Slievemore in the paintings on the walls there were no signs of life. There was no one. The sadness is on me.

I can tell you that they are all still alive, but they no longer live on Slievemore. The villagers had to sell all their livestock to pay the landlord their rent arrears. Nearly all of the poor things were close to starvation, so they had to go back to their winter home and live off the sea. Some, like Niamh and her family, chose the workhouse. It was a long walk on that lonely road to Westport. But she is still alive, Seán.

Seán was quiet for a while as he thought about his family and Niamh. Knowing that they were alive made him feel better. Then a thought rose up, a thought he had buried for a long time. Even though he knew the answer, he looked into Brigid's eyes and asked,

I'll not be with my family again, will I?

Seán, you will never be with your family. You are at the last stage of your journey, and you cannot go back now. Please know that you will see your family in your other lives.

Seán was upset, and could not bring himself to ask about Niamh. Putting his head into his hands he wept. Brigid waited until his tears had dried. When he lifted his head she said,

It is possible that you may see Niamh.

Oh, Jaysus, I hope so. I'm so glad that she's still alive.

Feeling overwhelmed he looked up at her and said,

Something's worried me since I was in Sligo.

What is it, Seán?

A small girl was sitting in the cart that brought me to Sligo. On her lap was the same golden ball that'd followed me and was in the temple. Sure, I know now that was yerself. She was awful thin. But didn't she smile at me as the cart pulled away. Her ma, herself and the others were all on their way to the docks to join a ship. Did she make it?

I was with you both, Seán. Yes, she survived with most of the others on board. Her name is Siobhán and she lives in America. She grew up to be strong, and named her first child Brigid. Siobhán will be important in this life and in your other lives.

That's grand. I'm happy that she's well, and that I'll see her again.

I am going to tell you things in the next few days that you need to know before you carry on with your journey. I shall start now.

Feeling a bit nervous, Seán nodded.

These mountains are one of the last, untouched places in this world. As in Ireland, and many other places, we will soon not be able to walk amongst its people. The invasion of the earth's soul will reach here, and the spirit of nature will retreat once more. Druidism is in your blood because of your ancestors. That is why you have been chosen by the Tuatha de Danann for this journey. It is a journey to accumulate knowledge that will be gathered from observation and experience. This will continue throughout your following lives. Others will be part of the journey. Bringing a solution to a broken world that has lost its way is the reason for all the journeys. When the time is right you will know what must be done to bring everything to fruition.

Knowing that this was a lot for Seán to understand Brigid paused. After a few minutes silence Seán asked his first question,

Bringing a solution to the world, sure I don't understand. Would you explain it to me?

If a person was put in a room that was in total darkness, then, after a while, they would imagine what was in it. After a long time in that room, they would believe what they had created in their mind to be true. This is what happened with human beings. When they no longer understood the Earth, they created mythologies and stories that they could believe in. What was once imagined, was later written down and, over time, humans believed it to be the truth. This is how religions began to guide the world and to assist the demise of nature.

In Ireland, the stories and beliefs were not written down. Everything was passed on by music and the spoken word. The druids knew that more understanding of the earth and the other world would come over time. They knew their knowledge was transient and would grow. To transcribe that in some way would have made their knowledge finite and stagnant. The universe, the sun, moon, seas, forests and mountains are all tangible and deserve respect. Yet humans choose to worship gods that are not tangible. Nature does not need worship, rituals or dogma. Instead, it requires respect.

Humans must learn, through empathy and understanding, the ability to connect with nature. They need to regain the knowledge that they have begun to eliminate. Through conditioning, humans have become willing to sacrifice nature. Your journeys will allow you and the others to understand why some humans manipulate others. When the time is right you will be able to enlighten people and give a choice to the world. Before that can happen, you must understand the human potential for good and evil. This has already started in this life, and will continue during your next lives. You will not be alone in those journeys.

Seán was looking perplexed, and Brigid said,

Do not worry. What I have said is within you now. One day it will all make sense.

You say I will have other lives. Does that mean I'll not be going to heaven or, God forbid, Hell.

There is no hell or heaven, Seán. When you die, you are reborn into a new life. Many humans believe in this. They call it reincarnation.

Seán's reply was simple and ironic. Jaysus, Mary and Joseph.

The things you shall learn cannot be taught or conveyed by books. Only through experience and observation can the nature of human beings be understood. From that knowledge it will be possible to see the fault line that runs through and threatens the existence of this planet. When you and your fellow travellers bring enlightenment to the world, that will be the day the light is finally brought into the room. Blind faith will no longer be needed. This is enough for now, Seán. I know you will think about what I have told you. Go and see Star. It is time for you both to become friends. Come back here when you have spent some time with Star, as I have another gift for you.

Leaving Brigid by the river, Seán thought about what she had told him. He also wondered what the new gift could be. When Seán reached Star he began stroking him and asked,

Where have you come from?

Like you Seán, I am from another country. I come from England and was taken to war in India by my master. Sometime later we came here to Burma.

Jaysus, you've come a long way like meself.

We have similar beginnings, Seán. We have seen terrible things but now we are free.

Will you tell me your story Star?

Star lay down in the long grass and Seán sat next to him.

I was born and reared on an estate in the Cotswolds. I was trained for the son of a Duke so that he could use me on the hunts. This was not hunting for food but instead killing for pleasure. This was torture for me as I was not born to chase and bring fear to other animals. I was not born to bring death to foxes and deer. All creatures are my brothers. It is the same as you being told to kill other humans for somebody else's greed.

When he became a Duke he joined the cavalry as an officer. He took me with him to India. It was an unhappy life because he did not have any love for me. When we became part of the cavalry he wore spurs and used a crop. We went to war in India and then in Burma. I was part of many conflicts which were mainly raiding towns and villages. It was often similar to the hunt only now it was humans instead of animals. It made me sad to see the cruelty that humans can inflict.

One day, on one of the raids the Duke was shot dead and fell out of his saddle. Knowing this was my chance I galloped from the carnage. I didn't stop until I knew they could not find me. For the first time in my life I was not owned by any person. I stopped to graze on a hillside when your friend Cormac landed beside me. Cormac told me to follow him to this place. He said that I would be safe here and I would meet a new friend. With this friend, he told me I will share a journey and then I will become free.

But how might you become a part of my journey?

I will take you to the places you need to visit. I will be your friend.

Seán was intrigued and concerned.

But Star, I've only ever ridden me friend's plough horse, sure I don't think I could manage a horse like yerself.

I will be your teacher and we will share control, it will not be difficult.

And what about your kit, the bridle, the saddle and the reins? We're after burning them.

The people here knew that these things were my prison so they took them off of me. I have no need for any of these things.

How will I ride you Star ? I'm used to riding bareback but won't we need the reins?

We will ride as one Seán. You just think about what you want to do and I will respond. Everything we do will begin tomorrow.

That's grand, I can't wait.

Seán walked back down to Brigid by the river. As he sat down beside her, she began to talk.

Since the world began, we, the Tuatha De Danann, have been the spirit and essence of nature. We came here from another place to be guardians of this world. We guide, but can never control humans in any way. As humans evolved, we watched to see how they would develop and care for their planet. People learnt to survive and live within nature. We were welcome in every part of the planet. Often, we took human form with many different names and guises to walk amongst humans, just as we did in Ireland hundreds of years ago.

Then, parts of this world began to develop in a corrupt way. It began to upset the balance. The dark, malignant elements that reside within some humans are not visible or tangible. They manifest as violence, selfishness, and greed. This element became dominant in some cultures. Over time, whole societies were manipulated and conditioned by these people. They became the Earth's dominating force. After conquering and subjugating other cultures, they applied the same manipulation. Conditioning humans over centuries has allowed this manipulation. Humans are easily conditioned and become dependent on it. Even though it is destructive, it becomes impossible to see the truth. The effect of this development in cultures has meant that nature and human kindness has retreated.

After Ireland was invaded, the indigenous people were manipulated and given a new religion. Following that, the spirit of nature receded. The oral history of the druids was replaced by a written history. In writing down those early stories, the Christian church turned the timeless oral tradition into folk tales that are like children's stories. The concept of time in the earlier culture was different, so that every story was about the present, not the past. This is unlike the concept of time that the world lives by now. It also meant that the stories could develop in the telling. By placing the stories in the past in the new written form, it took away their power and relevance. The written accounts are irrelevant and disconnected.

By replacing the culture of the druids with Christianity, they removed the people from their sense of time and the natural world. The invaders had learnt that taking away the ancient knowledge and soul of a culture was essential to implement conditioning. All conquering European forces applied this to their victims. Religions condone royalty, armies, politicians and the rich in their subjugation and theft of indigenous peoples' dignity and homelands.

What is happening here in Burma is what happened in Ireland. The results will be similar, but the devastation will be greater. Nature will suffer and recede once more. Religious doctrines tell humans that they are the only creatures with souls. This belief places human beings at the centre of the world and removes them from their place within nature. Believing this removes any obligation to honour and protect this miraculous planet. The world has declined spiritually but not materially. The consequences of that decline have been never-ending wars and the relentless destruction of nature. It is as if they are murdering their own mother.

We have had to watch as indigenous peoples have been abused throughout history. Countries that claim to be civilised have murdered them and stolen their land. These atrocities happened to people that understand the Earth's soul, and know their place in the ways of all life. Crushing them inevitably takes away an ocean of ancient knowledge that is crucial to the survival of this planet. This will become even more extreme in the future.

Turning to look at Seán who had his eyes closed, Brigid waited a moment. Seán looked at her and said quietly,

Sure, I'm ashamed to be human.

Do not be ashamed, it is not your fault, and it is not the fault of most people. Despite claiming to follow a spiritual religion, the people with power prioritise wealth. None of the religions they follow ever disputes this hypocrisy. Instead, the idea is respected. Consequently, the wealthy, the monarchs, and the dictators are endorsed by religion and protected by armies. In return, the rulers support the religions, and the armies are paid with pageants and glory. People are always convinced of the sanctity and authenticity of their own religion. Because they are conditioned, they willingly partake in wars, sanctioned by their leaders, and blessed by their holy men. In the future, even religions will be removed or marginalised. They will be replaced by the worship of material wealth and hatred. This will be even more destructive.

The sadness is on me Brigid. How would I ever be able to make a difference?

It starts with two tasks. One is to witness and understand greed and aggression. The other is to witness and understand beauty, kindness, and compassion. Other tasks will follow. Would you like to see that gift now?

Seán nodded. At that moment he heard a noise behind him. He turned to see an old monk walking towards him. He was moving slowly, and sat down on a rock close to Seán. Brigid said,

This is Yotag, he is the Llama, the head of all the monks of the temple. He is the link between the monks, the Tuatha de Danann, and the other world.

The Llama spoke in a quiet voice.

All of the monks in the temple are shamans from the villages in Kachin. They all have an affinity with the spirit world and each one of them has their own sacred temple cat. There are one hundred monks including myself. Part of the spirit of every monk resides in their cat.

Brigid spoke,

And here is your own cat, Seán. It is a manifestation of your spirit. This temple cat will be with you for the rest of your life.

Overwhelmed, Seán stood up to receive his cat, but could not see it. Confused, he said,

My cat, Brigid, where is it? I can't see it.

Look down at your feet. She is there, next to you.

Seán looked down and there was his cat, sitting calmly and looking up at him with green eyes. Kneeling down, Seán stroked her smooth fur.

Ah she's grand. I can't believe she's mine.

Of course, she is, said Brigid. She is a part of you, and will connect you to many things in this world, and in the other. Within her is the part of your soul that has not been marred by all the bad things that have happened to you. She will help you to heal from the pain of your past and will always be a comfort to you.

What's her name?

That is for you to decide.

The Llama added, Close your eyes and her name will come to you.

Seán did as he said, and in a few seconds, he opened his eyes and whispered, Angel, that is her name.

Both Brigid and Yotag smiled. Brigid said,

It is a good name Seán. It links you to your old self.

Seán sat back on the rock and held Angel in his arms. Lying like a baby, she held up her small paws in front of her. Seán could not stop smiling.

Yotag said to him,

We have given her to you now because you are going to need her very soon.

Seeing the look of concern in Seán's eyes, Brigid said,

Things have changed, Seán. You must go tomorrow morning, there is no time to waste.

Why, what's changed?

The birds have returned with news that the British and Siamese are moving once more towards the hills, but this time with many more soldiers. Flying in from the north, the eagles have told us that there is also an army approaching from Madras. If you leave in the morning you will get to both of your destinations and return before it becomes dangerous. Because the Siamese are with the British, they will be looking for the old temple that you are going to.

Seán was anxious.

How will I find our destinations?

Cormac will lead you to them. Three hundred years ago, the people of Kachin built a temple to honour nature. It is now just an empty shell. This will be your first destination. The Siamese still believe that it is used by monks, and holds the treasure they seek. This is why they are looking for it. They do not know that it was abandoned after their ancestors had raided it. The reason you must go there will become clear when you arrive. For three hundred years, something has been waiting for you in that temple. You must find it because it is important, and it is yours. After that you will go to a lake where you will learn even more. The people there will show you what they have learnt over many generations. Soon all their knowledge and way of life may disappear. Take your pack, fiddle, and food supplies. Cormac will guide you all the way, and watch out for the enemy. But now you must get used to riding on Star's back. There are a few hours before the sun sets. I will see you at sunrise. There will be food ready for you to take.

With mixed emotions, Seán walked off. Angel followed closely.

Star was lying in the long grass when they reached the top of the hill. Çormac was perched on his back. All the while that they were talking to each other, Seán was stroking Angel and Star. Star said,

Shall we ride now, Seán? By nightfall we will be ready. Angel, you must stay here with Cormac. Tomorrow you will be able to ride inside Seán's backpack. The first thing you must learn, Seán, is how to get onto my back without a saddle and stirrups.

Star stood up and Seán realised for the first time how tall he was.

Sure, I've never used a saddle anyway. I remember how I would be getting up onto the plough horse. But then you'd be a fair bit taller than himself.

Standing alongside Star, he grabbed a handful of his mane and swung up onto his back. It felt as if he had just flown there like a bird.

That's good, Seán. We will start at a trot and all you have to do is hold onto my mane. Wherever you want to go, just tell me in your mind. If it is not possible or dangerous, I will make the decision and take control.

Cormac and Angel watched as they trotted off through the orchard. Seán sat upright as he had been taught. Holding tightly onto the mane, Seán relaxed as they moved easily between the last apple trees. Once into the meadow, Seán decided to canter, and so they did. He enjoyed every moment as they moved smoothly and at a good pace. Soon they were moving as one. Star suggested a gallop. When the speed changed, Seán was pushed back by the momentum, and it made him laugh. Leaning forward, Seán grabbed the mane with both hands and laid his chin on it. The speed they were going was both impossible and thrilling.

As they approached some trees on the edge of the woods, Seán felt uneasy, and said,

Perhaps we should slow back down to a canter?

It is fine, Seán. I can move around these trees at this speed. You have to trust me. If it becomes dangerous, I shall slow down.

Seán's lesson lasted for two hours, and he enjoyed every precarious moment. As the sun was setting, the rider and his horse returned to Angel and Cormac. Jumping down, Seán said,

Jaysus, Star, that was grand. Tomorrow we will start our journey. Let's meet at the temple just before the break of day.

I will be there Seán.

Seán turned and ran down to the temple with his friends. One flying above and the other by his feet.

That night inside the temple the Llama told the people about the invasion of their homeland. Everyone was seated and the Llama was on the podium. He explained,

The birds are flying all over our hills and mountains. They are also in touch with other birds that live further away. They will keep us informed if the enemy begins to march towards us. Never have we been invaded by such a force. They have entered Kachin from the north and the south. To the west there are forces coming across the border from India. Seán will start his journey tomorrow. I hope that we will be here to welcome him back when he returns.

The mood became sombre as the spectre of the old enemy entered the hall. Seán and the rest of the musicians played music for the rest of the evening. The music was soulful and a comfort to everyone there. Afterwards, Seán said goodbye, because he knew he wouldn't see them in the morning.

During the night, Seán slept well and was awake before dawn. With the knapsack and fiddle on his back, he and Angel walked out to the garden. The moon was still bright, and Seán saw Brigid waiting in the garden. At her feet was a bag of rice and fruit.

Take this food, Seán. You are about to embark on an Odyssey that will be beneficial to you and many others in the future.

Just then Star walked up and stood beside her. Cormac flew down to join them.

Stepping forward, Brigid put her hand on Seán's shoulder and said good-bye.

He replied,

Slán Brigid.

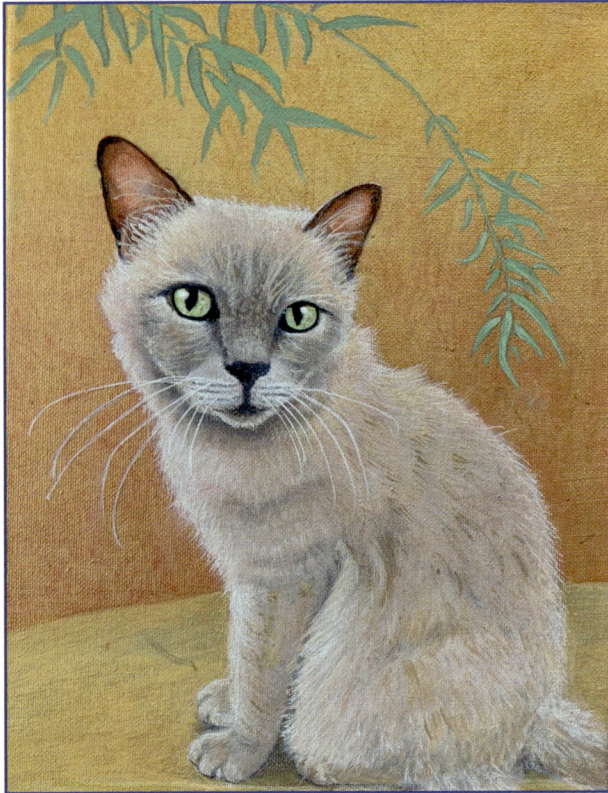

The First Endeavour

Brigid disappeared. After putting the food into his backpack, Seán watched as Angel jumped in. Seeing her sitting in the bag with her head protruding from the opening made Seán laugh. With his backpack, Angel, and fiddle on his back, Seán swung up onto Star.

Cormac led them through the orchard and woods to emerge onto a narrow mountain path. Cormac flew ahead, and, just as he followed the curve of the mountain, he stopped. He had seen something disturbing in the distance. After he had perched for a while on a rock, Star came along. Cormac spoke to them all.

Before you descend the mountain, look over to the hills. In the distance are signs of our enemy.

A moment later, Seán pointed and shouted,

Jaysus, look there's fires, can you see 'em?

In the distance, columns of smoke were rising in various places.

Cormac continued,

They are burning villages, and we must move fast to keep ahead of them. Much closer, in the valley you will see a small mountain rising above a forest. On the top of that mountain is our destination, the old temple. Go with speed, Star, and I will lead you to it.

Trotting down the steep track, Star moved into a gallop when they reached the open terrain.

From the backpack, Angel looked over Seán's shoulder to watch Cormac. It was dusk when they reached the forest. Safe passage was found along a path, newly created by Brigid. This took them through an otherwise impenetrable forest. When it became dark, Star stopped in a clearing,

We shall stay here tonight.

Before Seán had dismounted, Cormac landed on Star's mane saying,

Even though there are no signs of the enemy, you should not light a fire tonight.

To keep warm, they slept close to each other on a bed of old leaves. Seán rested his head on Star, while Angel slept on Seán's chest. Cormac did not sleep, but instead kept watch from a branch above them.

In the morning, Cormac led them to a small stream and told them,

The mountain and temple overlook these trees. The path that will take you to the summit is near, so dismount and go on foot from here. Keep your pack and fiddle with you, Seán. Star, you must wait here until we return.

Seán stroked Star's mane and said goodbye. Soon Seán and Angel were on the steep mountain path. Angel ran ahead, and Cormac flew past him to watch out for signs of danger. As they neared the peak, the narrowing path running above deep ravines was daunting. Seán tried not to look down. Near the summit, the temple came into sight.

It was a relief for Seán to step onto the flat surface of the mountaintop. Looming over them was the temple. Carved from the mountain, it was white and round with a patinated bronze dome. Despite being scarred and worn by weather and time, it still had an air of grandeur. Facing them was the entrance. Two stone columns stood either side of two intricately carved doors. Crumbling and eroded carvings of animals adorned the outer walls. Doves circled the bronze dome, while others flew in and out of small holes that punctuated it.

Overawed by the temple's beauty, Seán stood transfixed. Angel sat calmly at his feet. After he had stared at the partly opened doors for a long time, Angel rubbed her head against his leg and whispered,

We must go in.

Kneeling, Seán stroked her soft fur before walking with her towards the temple. Cormac was waiting on the ground by the doors as they entered.

An enormous interior full of shadows welcomed them. Growing in the walls were wild plants and vines. Seán could see no other sign of life, until he looked up into the domed ceiling. The doves from outside were flying all around it. Cormac flew up to join them. There was nothing to see below the ceiling except for a stone plinth in the middle of a dust-covered floor. The only source of light came from a big window on the right-hand side. Sitting amongst a few fallen rocks by the door, Seán rested. Angel was running around, exploring, when Cormac flew down and perched on Seán's shoulder.

Brigid asked me to tell you to play your fiddle when we got to the temple. Now is a good time to play.

Surprised, Seán took out his fiddle and began to play. It was a tune that he knew from home. One day in the future, it would be given words and called Danny Boy. Throughout the temple, his music resonated. It caused the doves to stop flying and perch within crevices around the dome. They were listening. As he played, the floor of the temple regained its splendour and colour. Layers of dirt and dust disappeared to reveal a pure white marble floor. Painted clouds and geese moved constantly around the smooth, white walls. The stone plinth was now draped in white satin.

Then, something even stranger happened. Calmly walking through the doorway and past Seán was a woman with a heavily lined face. It was as if he was not there. Walking by the woman's bare feet was a cat that looked like one of the temple cats. Monks and cats followed in a line be-hind her into the temple. Seán realised that she was a Llama. Walking over to the satin-covered seat, the Llama sat down next to a golden eagle. All the monks sat on the floor in a half-circle in front of them. Seán be-came aware that he was witnessing something from the past. The golden eagle was there to pass on a warning.

After listening to him the Llama spoke quietly to the monks.

Our friend has told me that Siamese warriors have found our temple. They are approaching and we are about to be raided. There can be no escape.

Holding up a small, golden statue, she asked Brigid for help.

We must wait and see. It may be too late. One thing is for certain, my friends. This is my last day with you.

In shock, the monks bowed their heads in silence. The cats became still, like statues.

Calling one of the monks to her side, the Llama asked him to take the statue. She told him to hide it under a particular floor tile. The Llama ex-plained to the monks,

Brigid's statue will be buried here until this world needs her help. Then Brigid will choose a person to retrieve her statue.

Knowing she was referring to him, Seán watched intensely. The monk placed the statue beneath a small floor tile at the base of a wall. When the monk returned to the others, the eagle flew off through the window.

Suddenly there was a loud bang on the doors. As they flew open a vio-lent force rushed into the temple. In disbelief, Seán and Angel watched as screaming Siamese warriors charged into the temple. Brandishing broad-swords, some of the soldiers surrounded the monks. The rest searched the temple. They found treasures lying around carved statues that were in recesses all around the walls. Their intent was to steal as much treasure as they could find, and then to kill the monks. Cruelly, they had decided that the Llama should be killed first, so that the monks could witness it before they were killed.

Wearing ornate armour, the headman stood behind the Llama. After raising his sword above his head, he brought it down onto the Llama.

With one blow he killed her. After that the headman shouted the order to kill the rest of the monks. Inexplicably a stone flew through the air and hit the headman between the eyes. Dying instantly, the headman fell backwards.

Everyone, including Seán, turned their heads towards the doors. In the doorway stood a formidable giant. Dropping the sling that he had just used, the giant moved forward and raised his sword. In readiness to charge, the warriors raised theirs. Pointing his sword towards the Siamese, the giant lit up the whole temple with a flash of lightning. Becoming frozen, the warriors were suspended in their charge. All they could do was watch this strange being as he strode towards them. Speaking in a voice that echoed throughout the temple he said,

I am Lugh, king of the Tuatha de Danann. I am here to protect these monks from your violence. For the death of the Llama, you shall pay.

Most of the warriors fell dead. Only two of the men that were stealing the treasure remained alive. Walking towards them he said,

Return to where you belong and tell your people to never come here.

Removing the spell, Lugh watched the men regain movement.

Still clutching treasure, the Siamese soldiers ran out of the temple. When Lugh turned around, he saw the monks crowding around their dead Llama. Standing over all of them, he looked down on her lined face. The monks had already closed her eyes and covered her body with the satin. Lying on her chest, and staring up at her bloodied face, was her small cat.

In a quiet tone, Lugh said to them,

You must leave this temple because they will come back. I let those men go because I know they will tell their people about the treasures in this temple. They will tell their leader that they were defeated by many Burmese soldiers, and that the treasure they brought back was part of a huge hoard. I have removed their memory of where this temple is. The treasure and the temple will become a legend. Seeking this treasure will occupy the Siamese for hundreds of years. During that time, you and future monks will be safe in a new temple.

One of the monks asked,

Where is this temple and what will happen to our Llama?

Tonight, her cat will die, and their souls will be joined. In the morning you must leave their bodies out amongst the rocks so the vultures and animals may return them to the earth. Then you will leave your temple. The eagle will lead you to a nearby mountain. Brigid has created a hidden temple and garden for you. It will be safe for hundreds of years.

Lugh bowed his head to the dead Llama, and then towards the monks. At that moment the whole ancient drama vanished. The temple returned to being desolate, dusty, and silent, as it was before.

Overcome by what he had seen, Seán sat in silence looking at the emptiness in front of him. Above them the doves began to fly again. Cormac flew down to Seán's shoulder saying,

Recover the statue Seán. It was put there for you.

Seán and Angel walked nervously over to where they had seen the monk hide the statue. By the wall, Seán found one tile that was smaller than the others. He knelt and lifted it up. The statue was lying there. After picking up the statue Seán turned towards the window so that he could see it more clearly. Removing dry soil from the statue revealed its full beauty. It was a powerful thing, even though it was only just bigger than his hand. Although made of different materials, it was primarily of stained glass. The dress was azure, and the hair was made of gold. Most striking were the eyes made from topaz stones. Holding it up to the light from the window, Seán saw the full beauty of the translucent colours. He knew that this statue contained the spirit of Brigid.

Angel spoke into his mind,

You are right, Seán. Her spirit is within the statue, just as it was in the golden ball and the white deer. Keep this with you until the day you die, so she may protect you. When you are gone, it will be looked after until it is passed to the next life that carries your spirit.

Cormac flew over.

Time is against us. We must reach our next destination before nightfall.

After descending the mountain, they found Star and moved on. Coming out of the woods, they stood on top of the hill overlooking a valley where there were fertile fields, and a lake that was nearly as bright as the sun itself. While they stopped to give Star a rest, Seán stared at the vast lake in awe.

Cormac spoke to him,

Our destination is a fishing village along the banks of this lake. I will go ahead and tell them that you are coming.

When they reached the water, Angel jumped down and ran along the sandy beach. Seán and Star walked through the water. It did not take long before they saw signs of human life. Just offshore were three, long, floating gardens running parallel to each other. Each islet was bordered by flowering hyacinths. In the gardens were an abundance of vegetables. Seán had never seen anything like it before. Nearby were sampans (long narrow wooden boats) moored alongside a bamboo jetty. The jetty also acted as a bridge to the first islet. Along the shore was a row of bamboo houses. All were on stilts with more narrow boats tied up beneath them.

Following a nearby path, they approached two rows of bamboo houses where the inhabitants were waiting for them. Standing close together and smiling, they called out greetings and waved as the newcomers came closer. When they were near, an elder with bright eyes stepped forward to greet them.

We are so pleased to meet you and your friends, Seán. Brigid and Cormac told our shaman that you were coming. My name is U Mung Lay.

Seán then met everyone else, both young and old. All were smiling and bowing their heads. The warmth and kindness these people were showing made Seán feel as if he had come home. U Mung Lay guided the guests through the village. Children and adults came up to give attention to Angel and Star. Near the end of the village, they stopped by a small bamboo bridge. The bridge led to one of the houses perched over the water on stilts.

After introducing Seán to the couple who lived there, the headman told Seán that,

These people are happy for you and your cat to share their house. We will take your horse to a field where he can rest and graze.

His new hosts were called Aung and Haymar. Aung said,

Please come in and see our home. You can rest a while before we all eat together this evening.

Haymar led them over the bridge and into the house. Inside there was just one room. It had been divided with green material to create a bedroom for their guests. The simplicity of the house reminded Seán of his own home. There was no door, just an opening onto a bamboo platform on stilts. The view when he stepped outside was breath-taking. On the distant shoreline across the lake were houses and golden stupas. Behind them, the backdrop was a snow-capped mountain range.

Looking out to this panorama, they all sat on the platform in the fading sunshine. Seán wanted to know about their lives, and they wanted to know about him. Aung was a fisherman. Haymar said she helped him with his work, as well as preparing and cooking the fish. They told Seán that in the morning they would take him out on the sampan to go fishing.

Haymar said,

We also work in the gardens with everyone else in the village. We grow our vegetables and flowers there. On land we grow root crops, including tobacco and tea. Would you like us to show you the gardens on the islands?

Seán replied,

Ah, that would be grand. I'd love to see 'em. Tell me how you have floating islands for your gardens. It seems impossible.

Our ancestors created the first ones, and generations have passed down their knowledge. All the villages around the lake have them.

But how would ya be making 'em?

Aung answered,

To make the island we must first gather clumps of hyacinth and sea grass, and bind them to a frame. The frames are tied to bamboo poles that are driven down into the floor of the lake. The plants grow and float on the surface of the lake. Once they knit together, this becomes the bed for the island. After growing grass on the islands, we bring up mud from the lakebed and lay it on top. Those mats become thick with about a third above the water.

Seán was impressed by how close these people were to the nature around them. When he looked across the lake, he noticed houses by the shore, as well as a sea of golden spires. Knowing these were stupas and being curious he asked,

Are you all Buddhists?

No, Seán. We have learnt much from them, but we have all that we will ever need. Nature is our teacher.

At dusk, they went out into the centre of the village. Lots of people were busy preparing food, while others tended to the fire. Soon the whole village was sitting around the fire, eating fish, rice, and vegetables. After eating, some of the men and women smoked cheroots. Seán was pleasantly surprised when he tried one with a cup of coconut milk. When he asked Aung what they were made from, he was told,

We use tobacco, honey, rice, anise flowers, and bananas.

Looking around, he became aware of how contented everybody seemed. The children ran off to play on the beach, and swim in the lake. People began going into the houses and returning with musical instruments.

A man sitting next to Seán said,

I am the shaman of the village. My name is Umung. Brigid has told me about you. She said that we should hear you play your fiddle. We have never heard such an instrument. When the music starts, would you play for us?

Seán was delighted and said,

Of course. But first, can you tell me what Brigid wants me to learn from you all. Umung knew exactly what she wanted.

You are here to learn about how we live. Tomorrow, you will understand what I mean, but tonight, please enjoy our fire, company, and music.

The musicians began. The unfamiliar music resonated with Seán immediately. After a few minutes, he joined in effortlessly. Music from the fiddle blended perfectly with the other instruments. A bond was created, through the music, between Seán and everyone sitting around the fire.

Early the next morning, a blue mist from the mountain covered the lake. Angel chose to stay at home. Wearing a conical hat, Haymar took Seán to the sampans. All along the water's edge, herons were standing motionless in the mist. In contrast, reed warblers were flying frantically in and out of the mist.

Haymar dragged a sampan from the beach. At the same time, Aung waded in the water beneath their house. He untied his sampan from the stilts. Both boats met at the jetty, and tied up alongside it. From the jetty, the three of them moved large, bamboo pots into Haymar's sampan. Standing in the stern with a long-handled paddle in her hand, Haymar gestured to Seán to sit in the bow. Between them was the row of pots. Standing in the stern of his boat, Aung nodded to Haymar, and they moved away from the jetty.

Seán was amazed to see how they propelled and steered the boats. Haymar used her hands and arms, but Aung stood on one leg and manoeuvred the pole with the other leg wrapped around it. It seemed impossible, but efficient. Because the boat was hidden by the mist, it appeared as though Aung was gliding through it. With his hands free, Aung tied several nets around his waist. The rest of his boat was empty.

Seán wondered how they were going to catch the fish. Before leaving, Seán had been told that he was not to talk once they had set off. After passing the jetty, Haymar stopped her boat and waited while Aung moved on. A short distance after he stopped as well. As the new sun became warmer the mist vanished to reveal sparkling waters. There was complete silence, except for the sound of water lapping on the sides of the boats. Aung was standing perfectly still. At that moment Seán thought he looked like a holy statue. Instead of being in a church, this figure was surrounded by light, mountains and water.

The illusion was broken when Aung knelt and picked up a teak dowel. Rhythmically, he began to tap the outside of the boat with it. Something happened that surprised Seán. First, he heard a whistling sound, then some distance away he saw a squirt of water shoot up into the air. He was puzzled. Between Aung's boat and the shot of water was a shoal of fish. They were thrashing about and coming towards them. Quickly, Aung stood up and was once again perfectly still. Only his eyes moved. The high pitch whistle happened again, now louder and closer. With his leg wrapped around the pole, he steadied the boat. Aung unfurled the net from around his waist.

Suddenly there were fins coming towards the splashing water. When the whistle happened again, Aung cast his net. In panic, the captive fish created chaotic silver flashes. He quickly pulled in the catch. Haymar moved alongside allowing him to drop the net onto the deck of her sampan.

Seeing that there were still plenty of fish in the water, Seán took another net from his waist and cast it. Seán heard that whistling sound again, but this time it was coming from Aung. To Seán's surprise they whistled back to him. It seemed as if they were in conversation. Meanwhile, Seán and Haymar filled the big pots with fish. Swimming just below the surface of the water were six dolphins. In order to catch any fish that had escaped, the dolphins came in close to the boat. Popping their snub noses above the surface, they blew water at the humans. Seán could see their faces clearly, and it looked like they were all smiling at their prank. This, in turn, made Seán smile. After a while they swam off. The second catch of fish was transferred to Haymar's boat. While Seán carried on filling the pots, Haymar and Aung turned the boats around and went back to the shore. People from the village came to help unload the catch when they landed.

Later, Seán, Aung, and Haymar relaxed on the decking above the lake. As they drank tea and smoked cheroots, Seán decided to ask about what he had just experienced.

I was after seeing dolphins helping you to catch fish. How in God's name is that possible? They even seemed to understand you. Did you get the dolphins to bring the fish to you?

Yes, Seán. We have fished these waters with them for generations. Each fisherman is taught from childhood by their fathers in ways to understand these creatures. They are as intelligent as us, and they have their own language.

Seán was dubious.

And how would you be understanding them?

Well, Seán, they communicate with their whistle sound. They combine and recombine these whistles to form a language. Because we have learnt their language, we are able to talk to each other. Many years ago, our ancestors were given the secret to understanding them, and, since then, that knowledge has been passed down to us through every generation.

All of the catches are shared amongst the village. It is the same with the crops from the rice fields and the gardens. We are taught from childhood by our fathers. Each village around the lake fishes with its own family of dolphins. These dolphins are our friends. If one of them dies, it is like losing one of our own family. We are a part of nature, and we have a deep understanding of the world we live in. We have a bond and respect for every living thing. If you look down at the beach near the gardens, you will see peacock turtles. They are always near. Those white birds by the water, eating what we have discarded, are white-rumped vultures. Elephants and gibbons live over there in the evergreen forests. All of these creatures are part of us, and we are a part of them.

Seán was surprised when he walked onto the islet because he could feel it moving with the water. They walked down rows of maize and flowers. Growing in the next two long islets were vegetables, such as pulses, tomatoes, cucumbers, and gourds. People from the village were working on these long rafts of bobbing vegetation.

Intrigued by the islands, Seán asked,

Will you tell me how the islands in the lake float?

As with the dolphins, the knowledge we need for these islands has been passed down to us.

Fascinated by the stupas and temple, Seán said,

I can see on the other side of the lake a Buddhist temple. Are you all Buddhists?

No, Seán. We understand Buddhism but nature will always be our teacher. We belong to the dolphins, lake, mountains, forests, and hills.

That evening, Seán ate with all the people of the village. Listening to the music and singing around the fire, Seán thought that he would like to stay with these people forever. Angel thought the same. As he watched the people talking and singing, Seán suddenly noticed Star at the edge of the group. Standing very still, Star was watching Seán. Silently Cormac landed on Seán's shoulder. Everyone could sense that this interruption was ominous. The music stopped, and everyone turned to watch.

The raven spoke into his mind,

You must say goodbye to these people now. There is no time to stay longer. Eagles from the mountains have told me that the British and Indian forces are on the move. They approach from the south and the east and are getting close. If we don't leave now, we may not reach the temple. Tell these people that everything may soon change for them. They are in danger and need to leave.

Although not wanting to leave or throw a shadow on the lives of these people, he knew that he had no choice. With apprehension, the people sat quietly anticipating what Seán might say.

Seán began,

Cormac has just told me that you are about to be invaded by a foreign army. They intend to take your entire country by force and have already taken most of it. We must leave now so we can get back to the temple. Soon the soldiers will come here, so you must decide what to do.

In the ensuing silence the headman stood up and spoke to Seán.

Your messenger has brought us sad news. Of course, you must leave but I hope one day you may return. We will leave our village. The birds will guide us. In our boats we will find safety. We have had to do it before when the Siamese attacked us.

Feeling emotional, Seán said,

I will always remember you all, and the paradise that you live in. I hope you may return to it one day.

Soon after, Seán, Angel, Star and Cormac left their friends. It was an emotional farewell.

Once clear of the village they began their race back home. Without the need to go to the old temple, Cormac was able to lead them along a more direct route. At one point, Cormac flew up to meet with other birds high up in the sky. On his return, he told Seán that soldiers were marching in their direction.

Along the dirt roads they would occasionally hear gunfire in the distance, or see smoke coming over the hills. Despite the danger the journey was uneventful, and they returned safely to the temple.

Informed of the home-coming travellers by the temple's eagles, everyone was waiting for them in the gardens. There was cheering, laughter and music to welcome them home. Star walked elegantly through the crowd and stopped in front of the Llama. Angel jumped out of the backpack as Seán dismounted. The Llama, who looked frail and unwell said, it is good to see that you have all returned safely. We have prepared food to celebrate your homecoming. After we have eaten, you must tell us about everything that has happened on your journey. After that I will tell you our news.

When they had nearly finished eating, the Llama said,

Before you tell me your story Seán, I would like to know if you found the statue of Brigid.

Yes, I did find the statue and I have it here in my bag.

When he took the statue out of his bag there was a gasp from all the people. Everybody knew the story and importance of the statue, but nobody expected it to be so magnificent. The golden hair and the topaz eyes shone brilliantly in the sunshine. The sun, shining through the glass dress, caused a myriad of colours to reflect onto the faces of the onlookers.

After talking about the discovery of the old temple, Seán told them of that glimpse into a moment of the past. His audience were transfixed by what Seán had told them.

In the following silence, the Llama spoke saying that perhaps Seán could tell the rest of his story that evening inside the temple. He said that he now wanted to tell everybody the news he had received that morning. The Llama seemed upset and vulnerable. Seán could see and feel the trepidation in his voice.

This morning Brigid spoke to me. She said that the enemy had discovered the location of our temple, and they were marching towards us. She has told me what must be done for you to make your escape. There is not much time left. You must prepare to leave tomorrow morning before they arrive. I will not be coming with you because tonight is my last night in this world. My work here is complete, and I rejoice at the wonderful memories I have. Between us all we have achieved many things in the understanding and appreciation of nature. I am proud of you and the temple, but sad that it must end this way. Leaving here is a sign that nature is once more retreating in this world. Soon, the world will be dominated completely by humans that are driven only by power and self-interest.

When you leave, the birds will take you from this mountain. Your destination is a village in Arunachal Pradesh in northeast India. It will be here that you will settle. Our enemies have not reached this part of India yet. Here you will find a haven with a community of people that are entwined in the natural realm and you will continue to connect with them. Brigid has told me that she will always watch over you. As you prepare for tomorrow's journey, will you please also prepare my grave. You cannot lay my body out for the birds because the enemy will see it. Also, you cannot cremate me because they will see the smoke. We will spend our last night together in the temple.

Despite being distraught and upset, everyone rose together to make the necessary preparations. A cloak of silence surrounded them that was torn occasionally by the crying of the cats.

Yatog asked Seán to remain because he wanted to talk to him.

Seán could not believe what he had just heard. As he sat down Seán said to the Llama,

Ah, Yotag, the sadness is on me.

The Llama closed his eyes and said quietly,

I know, Seán. I feel the same. Tsun wants to talk to you, and I must leave to rest in the temple. When I go, use the statue to ask her to join you.

Of course, but how?

What I was told about the statue when I was a child was that you hold it and look into the topaz eyes and wait. I will see you this evening.

With that, he walked off slowly with his staff and his cat.

After waiting a while, Seán did just what the Llama had told him. In a few seconds Brigid was standing next to him with her hand on his shoulder. She was smiling and said to Seán,

I am glad that you have my statue. It will be a part of all your lives. Do not be sad for Yotag. It is not the end for him. As you know, the enemy is coming towards you. It was inevitable from the day they invaded Burma. Now I must talk to you about what you have just experienced in your travels. Then I shall tell you about your next endeavour. You have completed your task in finding the old temple. and witnessing what happened all those many years ago. From this you have seen for yourself how selfish and destructive human beings can be when greed is their driving force. In your visit to the fishing village by the lake you experienced the bond that is possible for humans to have with nature. Soon, the ways of these people and others like them will disappear. Through you, the value of what they knew to be true will not be forgotten. Both encounters, along with everything else you learn through this and all your other lives to come, will be burned into your spirit. These memories will one day have a purpose.

Now I must tell you of your next quest. You will leave tomorrow morning with everybody else. On the second day, you will part from them at a crossroads. They will stay on the path on their journey to India, but you must go north to the Madoi Razi, the sacred mountain. It is a part of the Himalayas. Lining your path to a bamboo forest are magnolias. This forest is the boundary to the shelter of the mountain. No human being has ever gone through that boundary. You, Seán, will be the first. Cormac, Angel and Star will go with you. In this region the people have always respected the wishes of the mountain spirit and so they leave it to nature. Humans have never trespassed on the mountain or the plateau around it. For this reason, the whole place is full of wildlife. They live in a wilderness untouched by humans.

Seán asked,

But why am I allowed in there now?

Things have changed, Seán. The world is in danger, and it will not be long before the newcomers despoil this place. The spirit of the mountain knows this, and welcomes you as the first person to go through the boundary. Because the spirit knows of your journeys, and what they will mean to this world, you are welcome.

This is your last quest Seán and you shall learn many things, especially from the mountain spirit itself. You will understand how the world would be if there were no humans in it. You will be given another gift - that of insight, so that you may gain a deeper knowledge of the natural world. After you have all passed through the portal of the forest, the inhabitants will not be aware of you and Angel. You shall be invisible, in every sense, which will allow you to observe. This will change, but only when the moment is right. Until that moment, the animals would be frightened by your presence.

Seán asked, but what about Star and Cormac? Will they not be invisible, like meself and Angel?

Most birds are already completely free like Cormac, so he will be a part of that place already. Star will find there the freedom he deserves. When you arrive on the plateau below the mountain, you will part from Star and continue your journey without him. He will run free with other horses. Some of them have also escaped human cruelty.

Seeing that Seán was upset she said to him,

This is his destiny. Do not be sad. It will be an occasion of joy. There is a balance of predators and prey that has functioned for a long time on the mountain. It would be an unnecessary twist in that history to introduce a human into the balance until the creatures are ready.

For that reason, you will have no need for food. Your bodies will adapt to the cold mountain, so you will not need to light fires. All you will need is your fiddle and my statue. It is only a matter of time before humans invade this place and corrupt it as they do all over the world. Both you and Angel will learn much before you reach the summit. Also, Seán, you will receive more gifts to assist in that learning. I shall see you with all the others in the morning.

She then disappeared leaving Seán wondering what will happen to him after he had reached the peak of Madoi Razi. His worry was soon replaced with a feeling of excitement and renewed determination. Cormac, who was sitting in a branch nearby listening to everything, flew down onto Seán's shoulder. Angel climbed onto his lap and licked his hand. All three of them then went across the meadow to see Star.

Seán told Star everything that Brigid had told him. Star was so pleased to hear about his future world that he galloped around the meadow three times before returning to Seán. Seán knew then that there was no reason to feel sad, and that this was meant to be.

When Star returned, he simply said,

I will be outside the temple in the morning, ready for our next stage.

Seán and Angel returned to the gardens outside the temple and found the people still busy preparing for the next morning. Seán noticed that the grave had already been dug in the flower bed. That evening, Seán and Angel filed into the hall along with everyone else. Sitting quietly on the floor, they waited for their Llama to come in. Because the fire was small, and the moonlight was pale, flaming torches had been lit. Looking up at the domed ceiling as he often did, he saw that the nightly procession of carved animals were not moving. They just stood still in the shadows. All around the gallery, the doves were perched on the handrail. Yotag entered the room and sat on a chair in front of everyone. The whole room was silent. Yotag began to speak,

This is my last night in this world. I wanted to say to you all how much I have enjoyed my life, and how much I have loved sharing it with you and the people before you. I am proud of all we have achieved in understanding nature. Take with you the knowledge you have, to share with others in your new land. Please do not be sad for me. Instead, I want you to be happy that I am returning home. I will say goodbye to you now and leave you so that my precious cat and I can pass away peacefully in my room. When I die, she will cry out once. A short while later when she is about to die, she will make another cry. Then you will know that our spirits are together, and we are no longer in this world.

Yotag and Kacela stood up, and walked slowly down the passageway to their room. Just as he left, the flaming torches went out, and so did the fire. The only light left was the beam of moonlight.

Seán looked across the silent crowd, and the only movement was the dancing shadows from the moonlight. He knew the shadows were ghosts from the temple's past. The painted images on the walls had disappeared. Instinctively he looked up at the dark ceiling again to see that the animals were moving. Now, they were leaving the ceiling one at a time. Seán watched in fascination until the last elephant was gone, and then he heard the cat cry. There were gasps across the hall. A few people wept silently. They waited for what seemed like an eternity until the second cry happened. The soul of Yotag Rooh Ougji had transmigrated into the soul of his cat. Now they were one, and ready to go to the other side.

At that moment, moonlight flooded the hall, and the white doves flew above the mourners. A faint noise could be heard that was quickly getting louder. It was the sound of the flapping of wings coming along the corridor. Appearing through the doorway there came a great white eagle. Gripped in one of its talons was a glass sphere. Within that was held a small, but powerful light, the spirit of Yotag. Gracefully, the bird glided across the hall and up towards the opening in the ceiling. Drawing in its wings, it entered the chimney and ascended into the sky. The doves followed the bird into the sky to the edge of the atmosphere. From there, the bird would travel to the Sanctuary.

Moments after the spirit of the Llama had departed, four monks and their cats stood up. Everyone turned to look at them. One of the monks said,

We will take the bodies of Kacela and Yotag into the garden and lay them in the grave. While we do this, please remain here. When it is done, we will ring the bell so that you may return to your rooms. Tomorrow will be a long day.

Waiting there for the bell to ring seemed like an eternity. Seán looked around the hall. When he looked above at the ceiling in this new light, he saw that there was nothing left. The carvings and even the gallery had vanished. Only the mountain stone remained. Finally, the bell rang, and everybody stood up and filed back to their rooms.

That night, most people had difficulty sleeping. Some even went outside to stand by the grave in the dark. In the morning, everyone was outside at dawn, ready to continue the preparations for the journey. All of the animals were gathered and tethered at the top of the meadow. Many wild animals had gathered in the orchard and meadow. Above them the sky was full of birds, bees, wasps, butterflies, and moths. All the creatures were ready to watch their friends depart. The people were standing in the garden near to the door of the temple. The holy cats were lying together around the grave. Behind them, the humans stood around the grave with bowed heads.

Yue addressed them.

We are about to leave Lao Tsun. Before we go, let us all reflect on the home we are about to leave behind.

There was silence while each person became quiet in their own memories. After a while, a monk rang the bell for the last time. Moving slowly, they crossed the meadow to join their animals. Emotions ran high as they passed under the canopy of flying colours and between the wild animals. When they reached their belongings and animals, Yue said to them,

Tsun has asked me to tell you to turn around and face the temple for the very last time.

Everyone turned around and looked down at the temple. First, there was a deep rumble, and then they heard a thunderous noise. An avalanche of rocks and boulders rolled from the highest point of the mountain. Falling all around the foot of the mountain, the rocks covered both the entrance and exit. The chimney opening also disappeared under the rocks. While this was happening, the grave and the gardens transformed to become a part of the meadow. Evidence of the temple and its inhabitants had vanished. In disbelief and shock, the onlookers just stared.

After a few moments, Seán and Yue mounted their horses and began to move forward. In a shocked silence, the people followed. Seán was in front with Yue because he could talk to Cormac, who would liaise with the birds ahead. The order of the column had been arranged as part of the preparations. The whole entourage moved in single file through the orchard. Progress was slow. When Seán and Yue left the orchard, they rode on the mountain path, which was just wide enough for them to ride two abreast. It was clear that this would be a precarious and slow test. Carefully the rest of the travellers followed.

The Exodus

Leaving the orchard, Seán and Yue rode on the mountain path that was already familiar to Seán. Carefully the rest of the travellers followed. Soon the mountain was echoing with the sound of children laughing and babies crying. Passing the path that Seán had previously gone down, they came to another. A gentler descent, this path led to a valley of fertile fields. At dusk they arrived at a cluster of trees and decided to stop there for the night. Bamboo-framed travois used to carry supplies were dismantled, while the animals grazed. To make shelters for the children and elderly to sleep under, they tied the frames together. After that, they draped cow-hides over them.

The next day, they ascended the hills that nestled in the shadow of Mount Hkakabo (The sacred mountain). After flying ahead for a short time, Cormac returned and landed on Seán's shoulder.

Ahead of us are the crossroads that Brigid told you about. Soon we will be there, so you must prepare yourself. Parting from all these people will be difficult. Look ahead along the path and you will see the flowers of a white magnolia. That is where the crossroads are. Now look down to the lake in the valley. The town on its shore is Putau, and it is being attacked.

Horrified, Seán saw fires blazing in the town. Even high up on that hill, the faint sound of field artillery fire could be heard.

They may send troops up here to the crossroads in search of retreating Kachin soldiers. For this reason, your farewell must be brief. Our friends must keep moving forward along their path to India, and you must turn north towards the mountain.

Seán explained all of this to Yue, and the relevance of the crossroads that they were nearing. Soon the white flowers of the magnolia were in front of them. Seán was dreading the inevitable as Yue arrived at the crossroads. After signalling the column to halt, he dismounted. Yue told a nearby rider to go along the column and tell everyone to say goodbye to Seán and his friends as they ride past them. There was no time for anything else. He embraced Seán, and stroked the heads of Cormac, Angel and Star.

Looking forlorn Yue said,

We shall miss you. Your journey to the sacred mountain will teach you more than any of us could ever dream of. Your spirit is in us now, and ours is within you. Before you reach the mountain, you will pass through a bamboo forest. This place is the boundary between our world and the wild mountain. No human has ever entered it. You shall be the first, and hopefully the last. Be assured that the eagles of the Madoi range know you are coming to their mountain. Through Cormac, they will assist you to your destination. Remember this, the creatures on the mountain will not know of your existence. They will not see or hear you. If they did, they would be frightened that the balance of their world would change. Eventually the time will be right for you to be seen. Only Cormac will be visible. Goodbye my friend.

Turning quickly, Yue mounted his horse and started to ride on the road ahead. Standing by the white flowers, Seán, Star, Cormac, and Angel looked on in dismay as the displaced people followed Yue. For the second time, Seán had had to say goodbye to his family. It was as painful as it was the first time. The passing travellers were sad. Some were crying, while others just smiled. Sometimes, adults and children left the column to hug Seán, before running back to the others. The temple cats ran over and laid quietly in a circle around Angel. It was an enormous comfort to her. Once the column had passed, the cats ran off to catch up with their monks.

Watching them leave was hard. Seán and his friends turned and started the steep walk towards the sacred mountain. Far away, at the top of the hill, they could see the bamboo forest. A line of white clouds floated above it. Reaching up from the clouds, the sacred mountain loomed high above them. It was as if the mountain was riding the crest of a long white wave. Climbing a steep and rugged path was difficult in the midday sun. Flowering magnolias lined the path all the way to the forest.

Two days later, they arrived at the edge of the bamboo forest. Like green giants, the bamboo trees looked impossibly tall. The bamboo Seán had seen along the Irrawaddy were only half the height of these.

To escape the intensity of the sun, they stepped between the first smooth and straight culms (stems). Lying down to rest in the shade, Seán stared up at the distant treetops to see long translucent leaves wavering in the breeze. Filtering through them, sunlight bathed the entire forest in a constantly moving, golden, green light. When Seán sat up, he could see far into the forest in all directions. This was possible because there was no undergrowth or lower branches to hinder his view. The splendour of the forest reminded Seán that they had now entered the home of the mountain spirit. Somehow, he also knew that the memories of the misery he had endured were about to leave him. Angel interrupted his daydreaming by jumping onto his lap. First, she nipped his hand, and then she said,

If we leave now, we should reach the end of the forest by nightfall. Brigid has made a pathway through the forest for us.

Perched nearby was Cormac, who added,

I will stay with you, as we pass through the forest. There is no need for me to scout ahead because we are safe. Remember, the animals and birds cannot see or hear you. As you no longer need to eat or feel the cold, there will be no need for fires.

Angel led them to the pathway. Seán was riding Star with Cormac on his shoulder. Before starting down the track, they paused for a moment and looked down the bright passage to the end of the forest. As Star began to move, Angel jumped into to his backpack behind Seán. Moving at a slow pace, they listened to the sound of animals and birdsong filling the air. All the animals, birds, butterflies, and moths were in constant motion throughout the forest. Each creature added fleeting colours to the golden, green light. On that path, Seán's whole sense of well-being changed. It was as if he had returned to the young boy he had left on his own dear mountain.

Hearing Angel purring behind him, and being overwhelmed with joy, he shouted out,

Tis the beginning, lads. Ah, to be easy and free!

Soon after, they heard high-pitched noises. It was then that they saw the first clear view of some of the inhabitants of the forest. Looking up, they saw furry creatures leaping from one tree to another. They were a bit smaller than Angel, with thick, rust-coloured fur, and black and white markings on their faces and ears. Travelling in all directions, they seemed to be playing a game of chase.

The travellers stopped and stared in disbelief at their acrobatics. Seán laughed and asked Cormac what they were.

They look like raccoons, but they are bears called red pandas.

Seán asked,

Why do they have such long bushy tails?

During the winter they survive here because of their thick fur and those long tails. To keep warm at night they wrap their tails around themselves. (In the future the red panda will be hunted for their tails and sold for clothing in China. Deforestation and gold mines will eventually cause the pandas to become extinct.)

Sure, I could watch them all day, but we must move on.

Being surrounded by the beauty of the place gave Seán the notion to play his fiddle. Taking the momentum of Star's constant movement as his rhythm, he began to play. Although somehow familiar, the music was like nothing he had ever played or heard before. It captured the essence of the moment and the light. Moved by the forest, it was only now that a forgotten memory buried deep in his spirit emerged. It was a memory of how he had played in Druid times. Accompanied by the music, and in constant awe, the invisible band of travellers moved slowly along the path.

Beyond the last trees, as evening was drawing in, an open landscape came into view. For a moment Seán thought he was dreaming. Just near the path were families of snub-tailed macaques. Laughing, Seán put the fiddle back in its case and dismounted. The monkeys were sitting comfortably on the shells of giant tortoises. Eating from bunches of bananas, they sat chatting to each other. All the while, the tortoises wandered aimlessly, and seemed unaware of their passengers. There were even a group of baby monkeys huddled together precariously on one tortoise shell. Even Cormac had not seen such a sight before.

Needing to reach the end of the forest before nightfall, they moved on. Further down the path, a complete and utter darkness fell. Only the sound of tiny bats broke the stillness. Despite being nearly at the end of the forest, they reluctantly stopped. Settling down for the night, they watched a transformation take place. The biggest moon that Seán had ever seen rose above the forest. Drained of their colour, the culms resembled tall, white, marble columns. The forest became a silent temple. Just before he drifted into that sleep, Seán thought of his family and Niamh. Even though he still missed them, he was no longer sad. Somehow, he knew that in some way he was closer to them. Feeling calm and rested, Seán slept soundly.

Seán woke at dawn, while the others were still asleep. In the emerging green light, he lay thinking. Unsure of what to do when they reached the end of the forest, he decided to ask Brigid. Quietly, he took out the statue and asked Brigid if she would come to see them. There was no response. Soon the others awoke, and they started walking towards the sunlight at the end of their path.

Standing between the last trees, they looked out over an extensive panorama. Wrapped in complete morning glory, the sacred mountain stood like a sentinel. Sloping steeply up towards the mountain were forests of oak and beech. Between the bamboo and the first deciduous forest was a plateau of flowering grasslands. Noticing some movement, Star said,

Look ahead, in the nearby grass.

Just visible above the tall grass, a herd of small muntjac deer was moving slowly. When they bent down to graze, they became impossible to see. Only one of the deer kept its head constantly above the grass. Intrigued, Seán said quietly,

I think it's looking at us.

With that, the deer left the herd and started bounding over the grass towards them.

Seán whispered,

Tis herself!

Within minutes the deer was standing in front of them.

Through telepathy Brigid said,

I am pleased to see you here. Begin your walk along the edge of the bamboo forest towards the rising sun. You will come to a lake called Madoi Pond. It is also known as the sacred water tower of Malikha because it is from here that all the rivers that are the lifeblood of Burma begin. From here to the mountain, you will see how the animal kingdom flourishes without human contact. You will no longer need to ride Star Seán because you are near to your final destination.

Looking at Star, Brigid said,

Today, in the waters of Madoi Pond, you will become free. Thank you for assisting Seán in his tasks. Your part in his journey is complete. So now, to become free, you must part from your friends. When you arrive at the lake, and the time is right, I want you to swim in it. Memories of your painful life will wash away, and you shall be free. From then on, Seán, you will be on foot. Follow the lake towards the mountain to go through two forests. In this part of the journey, you will be given new gifts to enable you to understand your last lessons. When you leave the trees, you will be at the base of the mountain. I will visit you again.

Bowing her head, the deer returned to the herd in the long grass.

Seán and Star looked at each other. They were both sad, yet at the same time happy that Star's freedom was imminent. There was no need for words as both knew each other's feelings. Stepping out into the long grass, they began their walk along the outskirts of the forest.

Hovering just above them, Cormac said,

I will find the mountain's eagle and meet you at the lake.

Seán and Star walked alongside each other. Because Angel could not see over the long grass, she rode on Star's back. From the moment they started walking, they looked out over a sea of flowers that covered the meadows in the plateau. The power and range of colours was overwhelming. Amongst the flowers was a constant movement of animals, butterflies, moths, and birds. Like Seán, a nearby herd of small, hog deer was also moving towards the lake. They seemed to be unaware that they were being tracked by two clouded leopards. Watching this were several white vultures circling high above them. Several families of noisy gibbons hurriedly passed by the travellers, just as Angel heard something behind them in the distance. She turned and was amazed. She called out,

Both of you, turn around and look!

When they turned, Star said,

Seán, my dream is near.

Galloping towards the lake was a herd of fifty Himalayan horses. The sound of the wild horses was thunderous. Soon they were out of sight. Seán and the others now knew that Star would shortly be free.

By mid-afternoon they saw the dark silhouettes of trees ahead. Reflected sunlight was shimmering on water between the silhouettes. Drawing closer to the lake they saw lots of groups of different kinds of animals along its shore. On reaching the lake, Seán and Angel sat on a grassy bank above a small, white, sandy beach. Looking across the lake at distant purple hills, they watched a chevron of geese flying over it. Although the geese were honking, Seán could not hear them because of his neighbours.

The noise along the riverbank from where Seán and Angel were sitting was loud. Hundreds of water buffalo were either drinking from the water's edge or wallowing in mud. These huge animals had black skin, and intimidating pairs of long horns that measured two metres across. Seán could not believe how much bigger they were than the domestic buffaloes he had seen working in the fields. (Wild buffaloes are now nearly extinct.) Even though the newcomers were invisible, they still felt nervous sitting so close to this huge and imposing herd.

Returning to look at the bay of swans, Seán stared at the pure white mass of elegant beauty. Fourteen of the swans left the bay and swam together into the open water. Like flying geese, they formed a chevron in the water. After a while, they changed course to swim towards the shore. As they did so, everything around changed. It became night, the surroundings disappeared and all the noises ceased. The water now stretched to the star-filled sky.

Overwhelmed, Seán watched as the swans moved through the reflections of a thousand stars.

When they came close to the beach below Seán the swans formed a straight line. The central bird then left the others. It swam to the beach and came ashore onto the sand while the others turned and swam towards their bay. As they did, the daylight returned, along with the lake, the mountains and the accompanying sounds.

After looking up at her audience the swan bowed her head. It was then that Seán realised who it was. He whispered,

Good God, tis herself, tis Caer.

In reply, Caer said,

I told you that I would see you again.

After walking onto the bank next to them, she lay down.

You will learn much in the next stages of your journey, Seán, and I will help you. None of the creatures, from the bamboo forest to the sacred mountain, have ever seen a human being. Soon you will capture their attention. But please know, they will never associate you with the humans that transgress this paradise in the future.

Turning to Star, she said,

Your moment is near, and you must follow the lake with your friends until you see the horses. To them, you are invisible, and that is why you must swim in the lake. The water will take away your memories. You will become a wild horse, and be visible to all the creatures here. Your new life starts the moment you step out of the water. After joining the herd, you will spend the rest of your life in complete freedom.

Caer then walked down to the water and swam off. Without warning she disappeared. Star was shocked and overjoyed at his news.

Moving quickly on, they went to search for those horses. Skirting the buffalo herd, Seán and Angel rode on Star for the very last time. After passing the buffaloes, Star stopped abruptly. Looking towards the lake, they saw a white tiger with black stripes lying outstretched on the ground. The Bengal tiger appeared to be dead. When they got closer, they saw that it was breathing and asleep. (Tigers hunt at night.)

It was a surprising sight, particularly as the tiger was the buffalo's main predator. It is also the predator of all the creatures around. Seán and his friends moved on at a good pace, Star cantering by the water's edge, as they watched never-ending cameos of creatures at rest and play.

Pheasants and squirrels ran amongst the trees, while a group of giant, black bears played in the water. All along the lakeside were trees that provided shade for the animals. Predators and prey seemed to be in a truce as they slept, swam, and drank by the lake. The herd of horses that they had seen galloping towards the lake came into view. Because Brigid had told them about Star, they were waiting for him in a clearing near the water.

Leaning forward, Seán said,

Tis time now, boy. We must stop here and say goodbye.

Just saying that made Seán feel emotional. As he dismounted, Angel jumped down to be by his feet. Hanging his head, Star stared at the ground. Seán watched him for a few minutes, and then broke the silence.

Ah, m'anam cara (my soul friend), c'mere to me.

Putting his arms around Star's neck, Seán held him tight. Angel was meowing loudly. After a few minutes, Star raised his head and moved away from them saying,

Goodbye my friends. Thank you.

Walking into the water, he began to swim. Feeling sad and broken, his friends watched from the shore. When Star emerged from the water, he passed Seán and Angel, but did not see them. To Star, they had become invisible. Sparkling water fell from Star as he walked over to the herd. Standing close together, the horses were in a circle. Allowing him to pass into the centre of the circle, the nearest horses moved aside when Star reached them. After a few quiet minutes, one horse reared up, and galloped away from the others. At an impressive speed, he raced across the grasslands. Within seconds, the others, including Star, followed in a wild and joyous stampede.

Seán and Angel were moved by the spectacle. Their sadness gave way to joy, knowing that Star had finally found the place where he belonged. Returning to the water's edge they sat beneath the shade of a willow tree to rest and reflect. Nearby, the waters were busy with passing ducks, cormorants, and moorhens. As if on guard, three giant herons stood perfectly still near the water's edge.

Angel heard movement in a nearby tree. They watched intensely for a few minutes until two small, bright green frogs began dropping from the high branches. Gliding to branches far below, they landed perfectly. Watching these flying frogs was mesmerising.

Abruptly breaking the stillness, the ground started to tremble. Nervous, Seán said,

It looks like an army coming t'wards us. Can you see the dust rising above the trees?

Both froze as the drumming sound got louder, and they started to hear loud bellowing. Eventually the source of their fear came into focus. It was a herd of gargantuan elephants, moving quickly towards them. Having only ever seen small groups of tame elephants on their journey up the river, this was an impressive sight. As the herd drew closer, Seán and Angel watched as they came to a halt. Taking the lead, the biggest elephants went down to the water and started to drink. Following them, the other elephants were soon either by the water or in it. Watching them spraying water on their backs with their trunks amused Seán and Angel. Some were swimming, while the baby elephants played in the shallows. Others even swam underwater, using their trunks like snorkels to allow them to breathe.

Reluctantly Seán said,

Let's move on, we still have a way to go yet.

As Seán stood up, Cormac landed at his feet and spoke,

Flying here, I saw Star running with the herd. It was good to see him where he belongs. I have been to the mountain and met the eagle. He has explained to me how we must proceed. Follow the river up ahead that comes down to the lake. This river will take you to the first forest.

When they reached the fast-flowing river, they saw trees that had their roots growing, both in the water and above it. Seán had seen similar trees being destroyed along the Irrawaddy. He asked Cormac,

Is this a mangrove swamp, and are they roots sticking up out of the water?

Yes, Seán. The prop roots sticking up in the air allow the trees to breathe and be supported in the water. (These trees have a high absorption of carbon dioxide. The destruction of mangrove swamps to allow rice growing would have contributed in the long term to a poorer global environment.)

Nearing the stunted trees, they saw egrets perched in the branches with kingfishers flying and diving all around them. The prop roots projecting out of the water were covered in tiny, colourful, and glistening creatures. It was as if masses of precious stones were adorning the roots. They reminded Seán of the offerings he had seen outside temples, and on fairy mounds. Near the trees were what looked like translucent, honey-coloured jewellery. These small objects were spread all along the riverbank by the trees. Closer inspection showed that each one had static creatures inside of them. Most were the same creatures as those that were alive on the tree's roots. Others were bigger and alien to Seán.

Puzzled, neither Seán nor Angel could stop looking at them. Angel asked Cormac what these things were.

They are pieces of amber, or tree resin. The amber and the trapped creatures were fossilised millions of years ago.

And what are the big fellas? Asked Seán.

They are geckos. Soon you will see live ones in this forest. For centuries, animals and birds have brought the ancient amber here to lay by the roots of these trees. They have collected the amber from the shores of the lake where they have been washed up. They bring them here to honour these mangrove trees and the ancient trees in the forest.

Approaching the first deciduous forest, Seán and Angel realised that the trees were far taller than the bamboo, averaging forty metres high.

Looking back across the meadows for the last time, Seán saw several strange, grey animals moving very slowly. He had never seen creatures like these. Huge horns protruded from the front of their heads. Seán had heard stories of unicorns, but knew that was not likely.

Before he asked, Cormac said,

These are the one-horned rhino. In the human world they are hunted, but they are safe here.

Moving closer to the nearest tree, they stared in disbelief. They had never seen such tall trees, deeply furrowed bark, and strange, fan-shaped leaves.

Cormac said,

The eagle has told me about these trees and wanted me to tell you, Seán. They are called ginkgo trees and each one of them in this forest is over a thousand years old. Their ancestors grew on the earth over two hundred million years ago, before any humans or animals existed. They possess more wisdom than anything else on our planet. Even their existence will soon be threatened.

Overwhelmed by what Cormac had told them, Angel and Seán entered the forest almost reverently. All the way up this steep hill grew ginkgo trees. The trees at the base of the hill, with their gnarled trunks and outstretched branches, looked like the first line of a descending army, ready to repel invaders. Inside the ginkgo forest, the span of the branches created huge, verdant spaces. To Seán, it was an open and welcoming place that brought a renewed feeling of joy amongst them.

Going constantly uphill, they followed well-worn animal tracks for two days and nights. They watched herds of deer, goats, takins, and buffaloes grazing. Peacocks, egrets, pheasants, and squirrels moved nonchalantly amongst them. The canopy of the forest was constantly busy, like the bamboo forest, with birds and butterflies. They passed many small streams, and the sound of the river was always present. As Cormac promised, they saw geckos scurrying up and down the tree trunks. Below them, amongst the roots, lay pieces of amber containing their ancestors.

THE OAKS

When they reached the last ginkgo tree, they found a short distance of rough terrain between them and the oaks. Even though Seán knew that these were oak trees, he had never seen any this old and magnificent. Because the trees were so close together, and the canopy dense, the forest was dark.

Elusive animals and birds could be heard, but not seen. When Seán and Angel stopped to have a rest, they noticed unfamiliar trees growing amongst the oaks. Compared to the oaks they were delicate. Seán went over to one of them to look more closely. It was a tall, dome-headed tree. Its magnificent bark was copper-brown with peeling, lighter-coloured bands encircling the trunk from top to bottom. Clusters of large, white, sweet-smelling flowers filled the branches. Shining golden seeds and small objects adorned the bands. As well as brightening the forest, these Tibetan cherry trees were also the companions of the oaks. Intrigued Seán asked Cormac,

But what are these things attached to the bands? It's as if they're made from gold?

When they make their nests, the birds from all over the forests bring seeds and objects as offerings. The alchemy of the forest transforms the gifts into gold, and attaches them to the trees.

Jaysus, but how would that be possible?

Being so close to this mountain, Seán, means that we are closer to the other side. Anything is possible here.

When night began to fall, the forest became even darker. As Seán started to think that they should stop for the night, he saw a bright, moonlit opening at the end of the path. Cormac said that it was important to reach that place.

Approaching the light, they could see two cherry trees framing the opening. Bright moonlight made the golden seeds seem even brighter in this doorway. Dark oak trees formed a wall on either side of the cherry trees. When they got closer, a dream-like vision came into view. Cormac whispered to Seán, who was standing in the doorway with Angel in his arms,

This is the portal that Brigid told you about.

Beyond the portal, they could see a rectangular pond in the centre of a grass-covered clearing. Surrounding the clearing, the oaks created a perfect circle. At the back of the pond was a large black frame. It was the width of the pool, and contained two moons floating in an evening sky.

At first, Seán thought it was a painting, until he noticed the reflections of the moons in the pond. Knowing the sky was real, and contained within this frame, made it seem impossible. It was even more stunning than the golden-seeded portal. Suddenly intrigued, Seán watched a white swan approaching the pond. After dropping into the water, she glided through the moons' reflections. When she looked over at Seán, he knew it was Caer.

Stepping between the hydrangeas, they stood on the edge of the clearing. Looming over the oak trees was the snow-covered mountain. Daunted by its height, Seán knew he would soon have to climb it. Tentatively, with Angel and Cormac by his side, Seán knelt at the water's edge.

Caer swam over and said,

In this place you shall be given your last gift from the Tuatha de Danann. It will be your most profound lesson in understanding a fundamental part of nature. You will experience what is invisible and inaudible to all humans. Music is a continual vibration throughout nature, and everything has a natural rhythm. In animals, it is reflected in their movements. In birds, it is expressed through their song. Soon, they will share their music with you, but first, go to the sky and moons at the end of the pond.

Standing in front of the moons, Seán watched the clouds moving slowly between them. He realised then that the frame was simply a black line. Confused, he went behind the image and the whole thing disappeared.

Walking back to Caer, he looked once more at the moons and asked her what it all meant.

These planets exist a long way from here. In Irish myth, one is called Tir na nÓg (the other world). It is enough for you to know they exist and to store them within your spirit. In a future life they will be explained.

Seán looked around the oak trees and noticed that the portal had gone. Cormac said,

Seán, look up to the sky.

A bright, full moon was sitting centrally over the circle of treetops. Somehow, Seán knew then that something was about to happen in this quiet place. Looking back down at the clearing, he saw a huge, black bear sitting by the black frame. Seán was surprised, but even more so when the bear spoke.

Welcome to the mountain!

Seán thought,

Sweet Jaysus, he can see me. What's changed?

Yes, I see you, but none of the others can. It is not the time for that yet. I can see you because I am the spirit of the mountain, and I have taken this shape to allow us to talk.

Seán was speechless. Cormac perched on his shoulder, and Angel tilted her head to one side.

The bear continued,

It is good that you have your bow and fiddle with you. Soon you will know why they are so important. Brigid has told me about your quest. This mountain shall play a part in it.

The bear paused, and in that silence three eagles flew down and perched on the ground next to him.

Seán instantly recognised one of them, and said,

Nay, the protector of the temple, tis good to see you.

I have left your friends from the temple on their journey to the place where they are to settle. It will not be long before they reach their destination in Arunachal Pradesh, where they will be safe. It is a remote and mountainous place, far from the invaders. Brigid has told them about your travels, and they are happy for you. I have come here, Seán, to spend these special moments with you. These are my friends, Abhi and Ajeetbir, the eagles of the Madoi Range. They will always be close and watch over you on the mountain.

Seán was moved and replied,

Sure, it's grand to meet your friends. Thank you for watching out for me. I am pleased to hear that the temple people are safe.

The bear continued to speak,

Take out your bow and fiddle, Seán, so you will be ready to start your next lesson.

Seán did what he was asked, and, as he did so, he looked up at the moon once more. Hundreds of different species of birds were perched all around the treetops. Seán noticed that, amongst them, were many ravens.

As Seán began to tune his fiddle, Cormac flew away to join the ravens. Caer remained still and looked at him in anticipation. The bear spoke once more,

Soon you will be accompanied by a friend. Play, Seán, for this mountain and all the life upon it. Once you start to play, you will become visible to all the creatures, and they will trust you.

Whilst excited by what the bear had said, he was also curious about the identity of the friend. As he lifted the fiddle to his chin, he looked over to the bear and saw that he had gone. The mountain spirit sent out a loud, explosive noise that shook the earth and the forests. This was an alert to all the living things around the mountain and the lowlands below. It was a shock to Seán and the birds above. They flew backwards and forwards across the clearing in a raucous reaction to the noise.

When the birds became calm again, they began to fly in a continuous circle. Instinctively, Seán turned and looked at the mountain above the trees. He saw that the snow was now only on the very top of the peak. The rest of the snow had been replaced by a thin blue mist, which then dropped to the trees below. On reaching the trees, it illuminated the whole forest with a bright blue light. The water in the pond became the darkest turquoise. Remaining completely still, Caer shone in that dark water like the North Star in a black sky.

What sounded like a single beat of a giant's drum followed the explosive noise. The resonating beat rustled the leaves on the trees and made the ground tremble. Rising from the earth, the beat became a continuous slow rhythm. Seán knew it was his cue to start playing. As he raised his bow, a soft voice spoke to him.

May I start first Seán?

It was another shock. Sitting on a rock next to him was Cana. She was holding her harp with the strings made from her golden hair. Overwhelmed and speechless, Seán just nodded. Following the beat from the ground, Cana began to play her gentle music. Calmly, Seán took her lead. They played intuitively for a while, and in that time Cana shared all her knowledge of music with Seán. A constant stream of animals began to come out of the forest, and all the birds returned to the treetops. The first creatures that entered were herds of oxen and bison. Entering at different points within the circle of trees, they found their place. After they were lying down, egrets and doves flew amongst them and perched on their backs.

Other animals then followed. Giant tortoises arrived with macaques sitting on their backs. Following these were tigers, cheetahs, snow leopards, golden langurs, deer, blue sheep, rhinos, goats, red pandas, and takins. The musicians and the pond became surrounded by this unusual audience.

Lying directly in front of Seán were three snow leopards and four Bengal tigers. Seán felt intimidated by these enormous cats, all looking at him. To his surprise, and without warning, Angel ran across the grass towards the big cats. Although worried, Seán kept on playing because he trusted Angel. When she reached the leopardess, they put their foreheads together for a few moments. Angel turned and lay down between the enormous paws of her new friend. Seán smiled at the thought that she looked like the leopardess's cub.

As he played and watched Angel, Seán noticed something else near to her. Moving his gaze to the right of Angel he saw the shining golden ball that was so familiar to him. Once more it was in the lap of Siobhán, the gaunt little girl he had last seen in the cart by the river in Sligo. She was sitting between the paws of a Bengal tiger. Memories of the day of his enlistment flooded back to Seán. He whispered to himself,

Jaysus, tis the cailín óg (little girl).

With her thin dirty face and rags for clothes Siobhán looked just like she did on that day. Looking directly at Seán, she smiled. Her smile was also just the same and her bright eyes were still full of hope. In a hushed voice she started to sing a song in old Gaelic. After the first verse, her soprano voice and the instruments became amplified. Rushing down from the mountain, a strong wind created the whistling sound of ten penny whistles to accompany her. When Seán and Cana joined in, the song and the instruments complimented Siobhán's plaintive voice perfectly.

All over the mountain and throughout the forests the music could be heard. The song was a slow and haunting lament called Skibbereen. A song about An Gorta Mór (the great hunger). Seán had heard it sung by soldiers from Cork on the boat over to Burma. The entire performance was more soulful than anything Seán had ever heard. For Seán the song held the pain and sorrow of times that both he and Siobhán had witnessed.

Seeing Seán shedding tears as he sang with Siobhán made Cana smile. When the song came to an end every single animal looked at Seán in wonder. Caer whispered,

They can see you now, Seán. You are the first human being that any of them have ever seen.

Seán replied, how so? Why are they able to see me now?

Your new gift allows you to hear their music and for them to understand yours. So now, Brigid has made you visible to them because your music has inspired trust. Without hearing your music first, they would have been afraid of you.

Birds, butterflies, and moths poured out of the forest. Some landed on the backs of animals, while others rested on the ground in front of Seán's audience. The swans that Seán had seen on the lake came through the trees in single file. The swans formed a single line in front of the others. The falling snow and the line of white swans were as bright as each other. After encircling the clearing all the swans lay down.

The last animals to enter were two herds of elephants. They approached from either side of the pond and formed a line around the back of the other animals. Their formation mirrored that of the swans, but they remained standing. Seán's playing was enriched and inspired by the majesty of his new guests.

The butterflies were the only ones still moving. Whilst making a loud tinkling sound, they formed a transparent ceiling of colour. It was the same music that Seán had heard the wind play on the small bells outside the temples.

Fascinated, Seán watched and listened. When he looked across at the animals and birds, he saw they were motionless and as quiet as the falling snow. Slowly and quietly, music started from them. Synchronising with the girl's voice, the harp and the fiddle, blending sounds of the birds, animals, butterflies, the mountain, a ghost, and a human brought a new force into the world. There was a pause, and then the music became an eclectic mix. Led by the fiddle and the harp, the music spanned many cultures and periods of time.

At first, the music of the creatures in the clearing accompanied Seán and Cana, but then it reversed. Coming solely from the elements, animals, and birds, the sounds surrounded Seán. Wrapped up in that music were stories of hunting, storms, and the perpetual circle of life. Seán and Siobhán connected easily with this new form, and understood its language. Entwining with their music, they played and sang with Cara and nature.

Changing suddenly, the music became that of humans again. Instantly, the animals and elements adapted. The mountain beat became the sound of bodhrans. Supporting Siobhán and Seán, the birds became a choir. Now the sound of a hundred fiddles, uilleann pipes, whistles, and harps were playing. Working with intuition and telepathy, a perfectly coordinated orchestra had been created. The atmosphere was vibrant, and, when jigs and reels began, the tempo increased.

After a long pause, they played a lament from the future that Seán would experience in another life. This song called Caoineadh cú Chulainn was a child of all the traditional music that had gone before. Its power was so immense and moving that it nearly broke Seán's heart as he and Cana played it. It would have the same effect on him in his next life, whenever he would play or listen to it. That was the final piece. Seán, Cana, the beat in the earth, the elements and the creatures' orchestra, all came to silence at the same moment.

While they were playing, the mountain had sent an even more powerful wind. It carried the music over forests, rivers, the plateau of flowers, the bamboo forest, and beyond. It even took the music up to the clouds. Every living organism was drawn to the strange new sounds. Everywhere, birds and animals joined in with the music. It was an awakening to a new potential.

Seán felt as if his own spirit was flying on that wind. The music spread across the lands far below the mountain and captivated everything - except the humans. They could not hear it. For miles around, the birds sang, and the animals - both tame and wild - reacted with their various calls. It was the middle of the night. The humans were woken by the noise, especially from the elephants in the woods and enclosures.

During the last song that Seán played, he had closed his eyes. At the end of the song, he opened them, and was once more taken by surprise. Everything looked so different because now the snowfall was heavier. Every one of the creatures had become as white as the swans. It was as if a spell had sent them to sleep as soon as the music had stopped.

Still between the paws of the big cats, Angel and Siobhán were also asleep and covered in snow. Birds and butterflies slept on the backs of animals. The ducks, herons, storks, and swans slept in the pond that had become much bigger.

In the water near Seán, Caer was the only one who remained awake. She said,

That was beautiful, Seán. Now that you have learned to understand and connect with nature, I will leave you. We shall meet in your next life.

Turning away from Seán, she flew over the sleeping birds. Flying into the darkness, she soon became a fleeting shadow on the moon. Watching her leave was upsetting for Seán. He turned back to Cana. Smiling she said,

You have achieved so much. Now you must sleep. Tomorrow is the beginning of your final stage.

She said goodbye, and vanished.

Heavy-eyed, Seán lay down on the bank next to the birds in the turquoise pond. Watching new clouds moving between the two moons, Seán fell asleep.

At dawn, Seán realised that everything that had been around him the night before was gone. The clearing, pond, sleeping creatures and the girl from Sligo were no longer there. Even Angel and Cormac were missing. Only the snow remained on the ground.

Surrounded once again by oak trees, Seán stood, worried and perplexed. For a moment, Seán wondered if everything that had happened was just a dream. Perhaps he had not really passed through that portal at all?

When he stood up, Seán saw the black bear standing between two nearby trees. He said to Seán,

I wanted to show you where you must go next, and to answer any questions you might have. Remember that the knowledge gained from your lessons will not die when you do. Instead, it shall be inherited by your reborn souls.

Seán's first question was,

Where are Angel and Cormac?

Angel is still with the leopards. There is much for her to learn from them. She will return soon. Cormac has flown to other places that he must go to before he joins you on the mountain.

Seán then asked,

Why do humans not understand the rhythm and music that's inside everything else that is alive?

A long time ago, some humans began to believe they were superior to everything else on the planet. From that notion, all kinds of religions developed, falsely preaching that humans were the only thing on earth with soul. As a result, they lost respect for nature and exploited it. Because of this they eventually lost the ability to communicate with nature and hear its music because it was of no value to them.

Looking at the ground where he was standing the bear said,

Follow this animal track. It will take you to the edge of the forest and the base of the mountain. Leave your pack here, you will not need it. All you will need is your fiddle, bow and the statue of Brigid. When you are on my mountain, I shall be with you all the time.

The bear vanished. Without Angel and Cormac, Seán felt alone and uncertain. After putting the fiddle across his back, Seán set off on the track. Walking between the oak trees, Seán thought of all the incredible things he had experienced as a result of his new gift.

The Sacred Mountain

Taking a right turn, Seán found that the path changed completely. He was looking down a long, straight, and clear path with equally spaced trees on either side. The upper branches formed a continual enclosed and domed ceiling. It was a colonnade leading to a brilliantly white wall at the end of the forest.

After walking down the colonnade, he reached the opening. It was then that Seán realised that the white wall was snow, sloping up towards the base of the mountain. The powerful glare from the sun's reflection on the snow made it almost impossible to look at. When Seán's eyes eventually adjusted, he noticed something dark just beyond the trees. Shielding his eyes, he looked closer and discovered a bull elephant lying in the snow. Rising, the elephant came over to Seán and towered over him.

The elephant spoke,

Because the snow is deep, I am here to take you over it to the base of the mountain. When the spirit made the loud noise that started the beat to accompany your music, it caused an avalanche. That removed all the snow from the mountain and brought it down here. Now it is safer for you to climb. Only the peak still has snow on it. But before we go, Brigid has asked me to give you your final lesson.

Lying down once more, the elephant continued,

All of us living within the care of this mountain have been spared the destructive impacts of humans. We know what is happening around the world because of the birds. They are constantly in touch with each other and with us. Elephants have been used for hundreds of years to work for humans. This is cruel, and not within the laws of nature. Elephant calves are stolen from their mothers. They are taken out of the wild and imprisoned. Then they are beaten and starved so that they become conditioned. This makes them submissive and frightened. They are forced to obey and become slaves.

When they are older, some calves will be forced to accept the pain of carrying people and platforms on their backs. This is what humans do - they control everything. Since the invaders have come to these lands, the abuse has increased a hundredfold because they want to clear our forests. This is happening all the time. We can hear the cries of those calves in the valleys, and the death songs of the falling trees. The invaders have brought the idea from India to hunt using elephants. They fit platforms on the backs of captive elephants to carry them around. From the platforms they shoot tigers for trophies and pleasure. The platforms cause enormous pain to the elephants' spines. It also causes pain to their spirit to be part of the unnecessary killing and hunting of other creatures. Humans accept the things that are carried out by their superiors because they too are conditioned. Humans are easily conditioned and do not need to be tortured because they are content to be conditioned. They need to be led, and told what to do, because, over time, they have forgotten what it is like to be free.

Seán thought about his own people. He decided that they were in the last stages of the process of forgetting what it was to be free. It made him feel sad for them, and the rest of the world.

The elephant continued,

When these people come across others that live and survive alongside nature, they destroy them, or try to condition them to be like they are. These controllers have no understanding of their own world. They are capable of destruction because they have no love or understanding. Our days of freedom here are limited, and soon it will be taken away. This is why it is important for you to know and absorb the knowledge I have given you. With everything else you have learnt, what I have told you will be taken into your other lives and not lost forever. That is all I have to say, Seán. Your last lesson has ended. It is now time for me to carry you across the snow.

Standing up, the elephant gently curled his trunk around Seán and lifted him as if he were a leaf. As they traversed the fields of snow, Seán swayed from side to side, and could not stop smiling and laughing. Looking up into the clear sky, he saw the protector of the temple, and the two protectors of the mountain. They flew low so that Seán could see them.

After a long, slow, and exhilarating journey, the elephant and his passenger reached the base of the mountain. Placing Seán onto a boulder, he said,

The first part of your climb will be the easiest. By sunset you will reach a flat rock where you may sleep. After that, the mountain will become more difficult.

Knowing that the elephant would leave very soon, Seán quickly asked,

What about Angel and Cormac? When will I see them?

The elephant replied,

Do not worry, Seán. You will see both soon. Keep the statue and your fiddle safe. Thank you for giving your music to us, and connecting it with the music of nature.

Still mesmerised, and in awe of the elephant, Seán watched as he turned and walked slowly away. With the satchel holding the statue of Brigid inside his shirt, and the fiddle across his back, Seán started to climb. Initially, it was easy until the mountain face became sheer and more precarious. Progress became much slower.

As the sun started to set, Seán reached the ledge that the elephant had told him about. He swung himself onto the flat, frozen ground and lay very still. Exhausted, he closed his eyes and fell asleep. In that sleep he travelled back to the island of Achill. He was in the sky, looking down on his own Slievemore, the mountain he had grown up on. Seán felt dismay as he moved closer to look down on the village and his home. All the houses were empty and without roofs. He knew then that the whole village had been abandoned. As he looked down on the shell of his home, it reminded him of the gift of his youth - and Niamh.

Those memories ceased when he saw a group of people walking slowly, arm in arm, on the dirt road towards the house. In the group was an old woman, two men, and a younger woman. As they came closer, he realised that it was his ma, his brothers, Michael and Kevin, and Lizzie his sister. Instinctively, he knew that his da had died. With mixed emotions, he went down and sat on the rock outside his house. Knowing that he was invisible to them, he watched as they approached. Each carried wildflowers. One at a time, they knelt and laid their flowers on the doorstep of the cottage. His ma laid two bunches. One bunch was her favourite, wild violet. The other was his da's beloved apple blossom. Seán was unaware that, since they had lost contact with him, they had laid flowers every year on the anniversary of his leaving.

Kneeling at the doorstep, they said a prayer together. After, Seán's ma spoke,

Seán, me darling, these flowers are for yerself, wherever ye are. God almighty, we miss yerself and yer da.

Moved by what he had seen and heard, Seán went over to the doorway to be near them. Just then, Cormac landed on the wall across the dirt track from the cottage. Seán's ma saw Cormac at the same time and nearly fainted. Michael caught his ma in his arms as she said,

Sweet Jaysus, will ye look at the raven on the wall, tis himself, tis Cormac.

Flying over to them, Cormac landed on the doorstep. After picking up the stem of apple blossom in his beak, he flew off.

Smiling, Kevin said,

Ah, look, he's taken the blossom for our Seán, wherever he is.

Ma added,

Thanks be to God, at least now we know he's still alive.

Seán moved close to her and touched her face with the back of his hand. To his surprise she reacted with a gasp and said,

Holy mother of God, I just felt a touch on me cheek! I know it was me own mo mhic ó (son). T'was the boyo himself, and he's here now with us.

She was so happy to have her boy close to her once more. The others gathered around and hugged her. Seán was happy too, but also sad because now he knew that his da was dead.

While they were still standing around their ma, Michael said, wouldn't it be grand if Niamh were here with us now, God bless her.

They nodded in agreement and returned to the path that led down the mountain.

Seán woke up. It was dark, and he was covered in a light dusting of snow. He began to think about his dream. He knew it was more than a dream. He had witnessed something that had just happened. Michael's comment about Niamh worried him. He wondered if they knew what had happened to her. Not for the first time since leaving home, he wondered if she had survived, or starved to death in a field. Not knowing anything about Niamh, except that he would never see her again, was devastating. He just wanted to weep for her. But, closing his eyes once more, he slept until the sun lit up the forests and valleys below.

In the shadow of the mountain, he opened his eyes and saw two grey snow leopards. Lying very close they stared him. Seán held his breath and kept very still as he wondered what he should do. One of the leopards spoke,

Seán, do not be afraid, it is me, Angel.

Jaysus, Angel, how can that be? Are you after being a leopard now?

To understand more about the life of the animals on the mountain, I left you to go to this leopardess. She is our friend and does not have a name because animals in the wild have no need for them. I have called her Friend. She taught me how to transform myself into a snow leopard. This means that I am now able to climb this mountain, and Friend will guide us.

The leopardess then spoke to Seán,

I hunt at night, and sleep in a cave during the day, but I will help you because you must reach the summit before nightfall. This mountain is too big for you to climb, it would be slow and dangerous. We can only reach the top as leopards. You must transform yourself too, and become like us.

In shock, Seán laughed at the very idea of it.

Ah, go on, how would I ever become a leopard?

It is not difficult Seán. You have already become connected with the energy and power of the animal world through music. Because you are closer to the other side, your reality has changed. First, you must align your mind with mine. Before we start, make sure the satchel with the statue is tight around your neck and the fiddle is on your back. Kneel, so that I may see into your eyes. Then your spirit will align with mine. After that, you must ask me to enter your mind. That is all.

Seán felt peaceful and quiet, and, in his mind, asked Friend to enter. His eyes became heavy, and he closed them. It might have been seconds or hours, he could not tell, before he re-opened his eyes. Sure enough, he had become a snow leopard. The satchel containing the statue of Brigid was still around his neck, and his fiddle case was firmly attached to his back. This new body did not feel alien to Seán. His mind and spirit were still there in the new body. He knew that now he had all the sensibilities of a snow leopard, as well as its knowledge and power. When he started to move, it felt normal for him to be on all fours.

Friend was standing apart from them and said,

We must go, and you must follow me closely.

Turning, she ran at a high speed along the narrow ledge. They followed in disbelief at how fast they were travelling with such a huge drop below them. Seán saw that the path ahead became narrower, and ended abruptly. He wondered if they would slow down and stop. Friend did not stop. Instead, she kept up her speed and sprang off the end of the path into the blue sky. Angel followed, then Seán. The leap took them flying over an enormous chasm. Seán saw Friend land on a ledge, just before he and Angel followed.

Before Angel and Seán could marvel at what had just happened, Friend started to run again. Soon they were having to manoeuvre and leap between narrow rocky ledges. Their powerful chest muscles and long tails helped them to balance. Their ascent consisted of climbing sheer cliff faces, negotiating rocky outcrops, and leaping across a ravine. At one point they were in what seemed an impossible position on a ledge over a big drop. It was a dead-end with no way of turning around.

Seán watched Friend as she stared up at the rock face, and then, to his amazement, she jumped straight up into the air. All the while, she stayed close to the granite wall before she landed on a ledge far above. When Angel and Seán looked up in disbelief, they saw Friend put her head out over the ledge. Looking down on them she said,

You must do the same.

Both were reticent. Even though they knew that they could jump, it was still going to be a leap of faith. To their surprise, they both jumped and landed at the same time next to Friend who immediately started to run again. The climb continued for a long time, until they reached level ground. They stood for a moment on the hard rock surface, and looked at a green steep-sided valley in the distance. The valley sloped up towards the snow line that was just below the summit. At last, Seán thought, we can see our destination.

As the three leopards ran towards the valley, they heard the roar of a fast-flowing river. When they were close to the valley, they saw that the river ran down a grassy slope, and became a waterfall that cascaded into a deep gorge. On arriving at the bottom of the valley, they realised that the source of the river was a glacial lake. Frozen and glaring, the lake sat at the foot of a glacier. Soon they were running on the ice-lake towards the glacier. Despite the rigour of their journey, and the strong winds, Seán felt no tiredness, only exhilaration. It was an alien freedom and joy that he could never have known as a human.

Seán's transformation had given him all the knowledge and instincts that existed within Friend. It felt as though he had been born a snow leopard. As they raced over the glacial lake, Seán's new leopard senses were permanently receptive. Nearly every sense was arranged to help find food and be aware of danger. As he ran, he could smell, see, and hear the smallest creatures crawling nearby, or smell carrion over a wide radius. Despite taking everything in, Seán was still able to focus on their goal. Ice-covered rocks and debris littered the entire lake. Raptors screeched high above them, while a continuous wind screamed down the valley. Bouncing off the cliffs on either side of the valley, the noise sounded like the keening of a thousand banshees.

After a while, they were running up to the surface of the glacier. Despite many obstacles, they made good progress. When Seán looked into the pale blue sky, he saw the three eagles that were watching over him.

On reaching the end of the glacier and the valley, the banshee wind was left behind. Ahead of them now was an overwhelming vista. Spellbound, they looked at a huge white carpet of snow that was laid all the way up to their destination. Reaching up out of the snow, and scattered all over, were tall granite towers. To Seán, they looked like snow-capped cathedral spires. Aware that they were nearly at their journey's end, they ran with increased speed onto the snowfield. The peak became visible and Seán was surprised at how narrow it was. Running over the crisp and firm snow, the three leopards moved relentlessly upwards. Changing from the banshees howling, the music coming from the wind had become a soft and calm whistling noise. It blew steadily around the weathered cathedral spires. Eventually they reached the final, narrow masses of snow that had gathered most recently on a ledge below the very peak of the mountain. Friend stopped, and turned around to face Seán and Angel.

We have reached your goal and there is no room for leopards up there. You must both return to your own forms. The leopard spirit will remain within you now, and in your future lives. I will change you back, and then I will leave. Both of you, lie in front of me.

She put her paw on Angel's head, told her to close her eyes, and seconds later she changed back to a cat. Friend did the same to Seán and he returned to his human body. Angel rubbed her nose on Friend's and Seán copied her. Friend turned and ran down towards the glacier. Just before she ran into the valley, Friend turned and looked towards them. Friend said goodbye with a piercing yowl, louder than all the roaring rivers and banshees of the Earth. How proud they felt!

After a few silent moments, Angel said to Seán,

We must reach the summit before nightfall. We must leave now, but first, look down at what we have just crossed. Seán turned and looked at the enormous view. Moving rapidly, a cloak of darkness and shadow was drawing over the mountain below them. The sun was going down, and time was running out.

With a feeling of excitement, they began their last trek over the soft carpet of snow. Angel ran on ahead in what was left of the sunshine. Now they were racing the darkness that would soon engulf the entire mountain. As they got closer to the top the pure white snow seemed to be painted with a subtle golden colour. The wind ceased and left the mountaintop completely silent.

Seeing the peak closely now, they scrambled onto its flat surface. In the centre ground stood a large granite plinth. It was devoid of snow with a smooth polished surface. Angel jumped on top of it so that she could look at Seán when she spoke to him,

This has been placed here especially for us, Seán. It is where we shall sleep tonight.

Joining her on the plinth, Seán sat with Angel, and they both looked out at the far-reaching peaks of the Himalayas. Stretching as far as they could see, all were glowing in the dying sunlight. The scenery slowly altered as they watched the shadows moving closer to the tops. Enhancing this incredible sight, the setting sun threw a deep, golden light over everything above the shadows. Looking down from the plinth, they saw that the darkness had reached the snow just below.

Then, something unexpected happened when Seán and Angel turned back to watch the last minutes of light over the mountaintops. Cormac flew down and landed on the plinth. In his beak was a stem of apple blossom, as fresh as the moment it had been picked. Seán smiled when Cormac dropped the stem into his lap. Overwhelmed, he said,

Tis the blossom from me da. Jaysus, thank you Cormac.

Holding the branch, Seán said,

So, it *was* real, they really *were* at the house.

Cormac replied,

Your da's spirit has travelled with me in that blossom because he wanted to be with you.

Seán sat holding the blossom in an emotional silence. At the same time, with his two friends, he watched the dying moments of the sun. Usurping the sun, a full moon rose quickly. Clutching the branch in one hand, Seán stroked Cormac and Angel with the other. Being at sea with his da, was the memory he treasured most. It returned to him as he held the apple branch.

At that moment, the bright light that illuminated the mountain tops was replaced by soft blue moonlight. Cormac said to Seán,

Take out the statue of Brigid and the fiddle. Lay them alongside each other on this stone bed.

When this was done, Seán looked at the moon and the northern star over the peaks. He began to feel the sacred mountain gently reverberating within his body. Looking down at the statue, he saw that it was glowing with the light that had just left the sky. Feeling that Brigid was nearby, he looked up to see her sitting next to Angel and stroking her.

Smiling at Seán she said,

At last, you have arrived at your destination and completed everything that was required of you. The De Danann is proud of you. Tonight, you shall leave this world, but you will return one day to follow your next journey. In your next lives, you will not remember this one, but your spirit will carry every moment that you have ever lived.

Brigid paused for a moment. Even though Seán was saddened by what she had just told him, he was not surprised. There was only one thing that came into his mind at that point.

He asked Brigid,

There is something that I need to know before I die. Can you please tell me what has happened to Niamh?

Your darling Niamh is still alive Seán. She lives in a country known as Australia, and her life has been as wretched as yours. After you left, your whole village lost their livestock and crops to the blight and the landlord. They all had to leave their homes. Most of them, like your parents, moved to the fishing village you lived in during the winters. The rest went on the long walk to the workhouse in Westport. Many died on the way, including Niamh's parents.

Niamh was put to work in the workhouse and was barely fed. One day, the warden said that there was a chance of rescue for her and some of the other orphan girls. They could leave Ireland and go to a place where there was no famine. Niamh and sixteen other hungry girls were taken to a ship waiting in the harbour. They joined a cargo of a hundred and ninety-one girls on the Lady Kennoway.

On arrival in Australia, Niamh became a vicar's servant because she could speak English. A year later, she was put out into the blistering sun to clear wild scrublands with the convicts. After many years of abuse, and being burned by the sun, she ran away from the British authorities. To live and work with other Irish people, she escaped into the bush. Her whole life in Australia was far harder than it was in Achill.

One day she ran away again, and finally lived miles away from humans. She tended sheep and fences on a farm in the wilderness. (Four thousand girls from the Irish famine were sent out to Australia to be servants and bear children to help populate the new colony.)

Within your sleep Seán you shall fulfil the promise that you made to Niamh. But now it is time for you to play your music for the last time.

Without hesitation, Seán lifted his bow and fiddle and played, following the beat in his body. The wind from the mountain transported Seán's music to all the lands below. This time it travelled much further than before. Across land and sea, it reached his friends in Arunachal Pradesh and woke them. Coming out of their houses, they listened in wonder and sadness for, somehow, they knew this was his death song. It was to be Seán's last night.

Sitting with his legs over the side of the plinth, and the stem of apple blossom in his lap, Seán changed to a different tune. It was one chosen by his da. The song took him back to the many wakes he had attended before leaving Achill. In his mind, he could see and hear his da singing it at one of the wakes. He could even smell the open fire that Paud was standing next to. It was a song that he often sang at these occasions. Seán also remembered that it was the tune the stranger had played on the quayside as the coffin ship had left Sligo.

To his amazement, the memory of his da's voice became a reality. His da was stood on the plinth next to Seán, and joining in perfectly with

Seán's music. Paud sang the words to the air Seán was playing. It was called The Parting Glass. Both the voice and the fiddle were emotional, powerful, and plaintive. These were the words.

Of all the money that e'er I had

I have spent it in good company.

Oh and all the harm I've ever done

Alas, it was to none but me.

Good night and joy be to you all.

And all I've done for want of wit

To memory now I can't recall.

So fill to me the parting glass

Good night and joy be to you all.

But since it fell into my lot

That I should rise, and you should not

I'll gently rise and softly call

Good night and joy be to you all

The Parting Glass filled the air across mountains and valleys. When the song finished, Seán's da disappeared. Now still and silent, Seán wished he could have held his da's hand, as he did when he was a child. Still, he was comforted to know his da's spirit was with him.

Laying her hand on Seán's shoulder Brigid said,

Now, you must lay the fiddle, bow, case, statue, and satchel in the snow below the plinth.

After he had done this, Seán knew it was time for him to sleep. Angel and Cormac were at the end of his bed as he lay down. After he had closed his eyes, Angel walked along his body and lay on his chest. As always, he became relaxed when he heard her purring. Holding the branch of apple blossom, he closed his eyes and thought about what Brigid had said earlier,

Soon you shall fulfil the promise that you made Niamh.

He wondered what that promise was.

Opening his eyes, he looked up from his now snow-covered bed at the stars and felt connected to them all.

When he closed his eyes once more, he and Angel fell into a deep sleep. It was then that his spirit stepped out of his sleeping body. Standing next to the plinth, Seán became his sixteen-year-old self again. He started to search what had now become the dawn twilight, but did not know what he was looking and waiting for.

A mere moment before Seán's spirit had looked up at the sky, thousands of miles away in a small, isolated shack, a woman was sleeping. Inside her home was a chair, a straw bed, and a dirt floor. Outside in the yard was her horse, and a small water hole. A tiny speck in a never-ending outback. It was Niamh that slept, and dreamt on her bed of straw. In her dream, she heard the music, and the singing of the Parting Glass, and she knew who was playing and singing.

As hope entered her mind, her spirit stepped outside of its sleeping body, and walked towards the door. Niamh, too, had become just sixteen years old, and dressed as she was on the day she said goodbye to Seán. Niamh's cropped, sun-bleached hair was once again long and wavy. Its colour had returned to that golden red of her youth. Replacing her lined and sun-damaged skin, Niamh's soft, country skin had returned.

She stepped lightly through the cabin door, and into the heat of the night. Her only friend was standing in the yard outside. It was a black horse with a white star between his eyes. First, she stroked his nose to say goodbye, and then she stretched her arms towards the sky. Niamh rose into the black sky. As a bright shooting star, she travelled over continents towards the Himalayas.

As that shooting star approached the Madoi range, Niamh transformed herself into a swallow, and glided through the falling snow. The dark bird contrasted with the snow, allowing Seán to see her as she flew towards him. He knew it was Niamh. Landing close to Seán, the swallow changed back into the young girl he loved. Both were smiling and tearful as they embraced.

In perfect contentment, Seán said,

Ah, Niamh, I said we'd be together one day, and here we are.

She answered,

So you did, Seán, but there's another promise you made to me. You said you'd come back to Slievemore.

Jaysus, I'm sorry Niamh, I would never have been able to.

Niamh interrupted him by saying,

Whisht now, we can still go home, and then your promise will come true. Let's close our eyes and hold hands. Will we step over this edge and see where it takes us?

With a leap of faith, they stepped into the air, and in seconds were in Slievemore. Opening their eyes, they found themselves in the field above their homes. Sitting on the grass the teenagers watched the day breaking over the Atlantic. Thunder suddenly tore into the silence and was followed by a bolt of forked lightning. Descending from the dark ceiling of clouds it pierced the dawn sky to touch the horizon. Emanating from that point an explosion of incandescant light briefly covered the sky, sea and mountainside.

Moving closer together, Seán and Niamh talked about their lives before the An gorta Mor.

Drifting up from their village below the peat fires filled the air with its aroma and embraced them. Being an everyday part of their childhood, it served to reinforce their memories.

Eventually, Seán said,

We'll share new lives after this one. I don't know anything about 'em, but I do know that in one of 'em we'll be together. And by God I'll make a decent woman of yer!

She laughed and said,

Well now that's awful kind of yer, Mister O'Malley. I'll be looking forward to that!

Reluctantly, Seán said,

We must go back to my sleeping body, a chuisle mo chroi. Tis nearly time for us to end our journey and leave this world.

As the warmth of the sun reached them they closed their eyes. When they re-opened them they were standing next to the plinth on the snow-capped mountain.

Holding each other's hands, Seán and Niamh leant forward. She lay her cheek on top of Angel's head and stroked her. Seán's spirit brushed the light dusting of snow from his body's eyelids.

Angel awoke. Purring, she sat up and looked at the spirits. There were no words, just a last caress between the two lovers. As they enjoyed their last moments together, all three closed their eyes, and a frail voice came out of the darkness saying,

Seán, can ya hear me looking at ya?

With great joy, Seán's spirit answered his grandma,

Oh, I can indeed!

Well, tis time a mhic. Kiss your darling now, and the both of youse come over here to the other side.

Seán looked over at Angel, who was staring at both of them, and then he looked at Niamh. The young lovers kissed, and in that precious moment, Seán and Niamh died.

Seán's spirit returned to his dead body, while Niamh's became a small bright light on one of Seán's closed eyelids. Angel lay back down on Seán's chest to wait for the moment of her own death and transmigration. The little branch held in Seán's hand let go of its blossom, which scattered over the mountainside. All the while, Cormac sat like a statue at the end of the stone slab, watching and waiting.

There was complete silence in the following minutes, until it was broken by Angel as she began to wail. It was the sound of the keening that had followed Seán when he left his village. This was Angel's death song, and, when she died, Seán's soul travelled into hers and the two became one. That single soul became a bright light on the eyelid across from the one that held Niamh's.

Cormac's earthly task was about to be completed too, and he changed into a white, spirit bird. Cormac was to take the souls to the Sanctuary where they would rest on the other side. Hovering over Seán's face, Cormac, the spirit bird, lifted the luminous souls. Rising into the sky, they passed through a gathering of white vultures waiting patiently for the souls to leave. Once Cormac and the two souls had risen above them, the white vultures circled once, before dropping like ghosts through the snow.

It was their role to complete the last part of Seán's journey on earth - to return Seán and Angels' bodies to nature.

Above the vultures, the spirit bird passed through another ceiling of circling birds. These were eagles that had gathered from the other mountains to witness Seán's last moments. Cormac passed through them. Like a cortege, the eagles accompanied the departing spirits to the end of the atmosphere. When they reached that point, the spirit bird vanished, and travelled to another dimension in less than a second.

The bird and the two spirits approached the Sanctuary. It was here that they would wait with all the other spirits that would share their mission. The Sanctuary resembled an austere and enormous face. Leading up to the entrance was a line of white birds. Each one was a spirit bird that belong to the Sanctuary. Their purpose was to take their spirit to Earth whenever the time was right. There they would protect their charge.

Cormac took Seán and Niamh inside the Sanctuary and left them to join the line of spirit birds. At the same time the cortege of eagles returned to the Himalayas where they dispersed to return to their own mountains. All except Nay, the guardian of the temple. Flying down to the mountain-top for the fiddle and statue, he swooped as if they were his prey. Picking up the case and satchel in his talons, Nay flew off to the Llama in Arunachal Pradesh, where the statue and fiddle would be kept safe until they were needed again.

In that small shack in the outback, Niamh's body still lay on the straw bed. It was daybreak, and her horse had wandered in through the open door to stand over her. In the confines of that shack, Niamh's life of hardship and heartbreak were tangible. Yet, on this bright morning, there was one thing that contradicted all - Niamh's face. The lifeless sixteen-year-old had a smile to outshine the sun itself. At last, Niamh and Seán were le chéile (together).